Rourke faced her. "

Lisa did a credible job of hiding her astonishment. "And you want the institute to assist with that? We have an excellent history with surrogacy."

"I know."

Relief coursed through her. He'd said he wanted an heir. A child. They could help to make that come about. "Confidentiality is sacred at the Armstrong Institute, Rourke. You don't have to worry about that. As for the surrogate, if you have someone in mind, our attorney will walk through the entire process with both of you. And if you don't have someone in mind, we have—"

"I do. You."

It took her a minute to realize what he'd said. She pressed her hand to her chest, a disbelieving laugh on her lips. "You want *me* to be your surrogate?"

"No. I want you to be my wife."

Dear Reader,

I've said more than once how much I enjoy participating
in multiauthor continuities. I have the chance to work
with—and learn from—authors whose work I admire,
and sometimes work again with authors I've had such
fun with on previous projects. THE BABY CHASE
has been no exception. It has also given me a chance to
work again with editor extraordinaire Susan Litman who
somehow manages to keep tabs on a mountain of details
(a mammoth-size task that would send me around the
bend) and does it with such amazing humor and grace.

So welcome, again, to the Armstrong Fertility Institute,
where families are made and where the Armstrong
family, in particular, learns just how much of a family
they really can be.

I hope you enjoy the chase!

Allison Leigh

THE
BILLIONAIRE'S
BABY PLAN

ALLISON LEIGH

Silhouette®

SPECIAL EDITION®

Published by Silhouette Books

America's Publisher of Contemporary Romance

 SILHOUETTE BOOKS

ISBN-13: 978-0-373-65530-4

Recycling programs for this product may not exist in your area.

THE BILLIONAIRE'S BABY PLAN

Visit Silhouette Books at www.eHarlequin.com

Printed in U.S.A.

ALLISON LEIGH

started early by writing a Halloween play that her grade-school class performed. Since then, though her tastes have changed, her love for reading has not. And her writing appetite simply grows more voracious by the day.

She has been a finalist for a RITA® Award and a Holt Medallion. But the true highlight of her day as a writer is when she receives word from a reader that they laughed, cried or lost a night of sleep while reading one of her books.

Born in Southern California, Allison has lived in several different cities in four different states. She has been, at one time or another, a cosmetologist, a computer programmer and a secretary. She has recently begun writing full-time after spending nearly a decade as an administrative assistant for a busy neighborhood church. She currently makes her home in Arizona with her family. She loves to hear from her readers, who can write to her at P.O. Box 40772, Mesa, AZ 85274-0772.

For my husband.

Prologue

"Good news." Lisa Armstrong sailed into the living room of her brother Paul's Beacon Hill town house, waving a newspaper over her head like a flag. "All of that sweet-talking to the features editor I've been doing the past few months are finally paying off. The paper's going to do a twelve-week series on families seeking alternative methods of conceiving, and the Armstrong Fertility Institute is going to be prominently featured." She felt her brilliant smile wilt a little when she finally focused on her brother's unsmiling expression. "This is good news," she reminded him. Her gaze switched to Ramona Tate's pretty face. "All human interest and all *good* press for the clinic. Nothing for you to have to spin into something more palatable."

But Ramona did not look overjoyed, and as the institute's public-relations magician—not to mention her brother's fiancée—she ought to have, particularly considering the tap-dancing she'd been having to do for too long now.

Lisa slowly lowered the paper and tossed it onto the coffee table. She'd been a little late to the sudden gathering her brother had called, and his spacious living room suddenly felt as if it was closing in on her.

Thoughts that her brother and Ramona had called the get-together to announce that they'd finally set a date for their wedding fizzled. There wasn't a speck of joy on the faces of any of the handful of people gathered there.

She looked back at Paul. "What's happened?"

"Derek has resigned his position as CFO of the institute." Paul's voice was even, but oddly flat.

"*What?* Why?"

"The financial audit that Harvey Nordinger conducted turned up serious discrepancies."

"Which, as CFO, our silver-tongued brother should be dealing with," she countered readily. She already knew the audit that Paul had instigated had shown less than satisfactory results.

Paul's lips twisted. "*I* told Derek to resign, Lis."

She felt the air leave her lungs in a whoosh. She sank down onto the arm of the couch, staring. "But he's part of this family." And the family *was* the institute. It had been since their obstetrician father, Gerald, had established it more than two decades earlier, expanding it from its roots as an innovative fertility clinic into one of the world's premier biotech firms in the areas of infertility and genetic testing.

Paul, the eldest, was chief of staff. Derek, Paul's twin, served as the CFO and Lisa, the youngest, was the administrator. Only Olivia, their other sibling, remained uninvolved in the day-to-day operations of the clinic.

Paul let out a rough sigh and raked his fingers through his hair. He shared a look with Ramona. "If Derek weren't family, we'd be prosecuting him."

Lisa blinked. "Excuse me?"

"He's been embezzling from the institute. Harvey's proved it."

She gave a disbelieving laugh. "Harvey's wrong. I know you trust him implicitly, Paul, but he's wrong." She looked around the room, from face to face. Ted Bonner and Chance Demetrios, the shining duo that Paul had lured away from San Francisco to head up their research operation. Sara Beth, who was not only the institute's head nurse, but also Lisa's best friend and Ted's bride. They all, along with Ramona, were eyeing Lisa with something akin to pity. "He has to be," she insisted. Derek might be Paul's twin, but she was the one who felt closest to him.

And everyone there knew it.

Unease was blooming in her throat. Derek had his faults, certainly. But they all did. And most of those faults were centered on their unswerving commitment to the institute. "Derek wouldn't steal from his own family."

"I'm sorry, Lisa. He—" Paul broke off, his jaw clenching. Ramona slid her slender hand over his shoulder and his jaw slowly eased. His hand covered Ramona's. "He admitted it," he finished gruffly.

His words fell like stones.

Lisa's throat slowly tightened and her nose started to burn. She wanted to argue.

To convince him that, somehow, it was a terrible mistake. But how could she? The truth was written on his face.

He cleared his throat. "The reason why I wanted everyone to meet here, instead of at the institute, is because I want to make certain none of this gets out. Not to any of the staff or the patients, but especially not the media or—"

"Daddy," she finished, her voice going hoarse. Until his declining health had forced his retirement, the Armstrong Fertility Institute had been Gerald Armstrong's life. "He can't find out. It'll kill him."

"Which brings us to the next point of all of this." Lisa didn't see how it was possible, but Paul looked even grimmer. "Finances. We barely have enough operating capital left to keep our doors open through the quarter. As it is, we'll have to cut our budgets to the bone. If we lay off—"

"*No.*" Lisa shoved off the couch like a shot, wrapping her arms around her waist. "The second anyone gets wind of layoffs, the reporters will be back on us like sharks." She shook her head. "Only this time they'll have real blood to find. There has to be other ways for us to cut expenses. I don't know about everyone else, but I'll stop taking a salary—"

"Lisa—"

She ignored him. "—and we'll get together a prospectus. We'll get a loan."

"No bank is going to touch us in the condition we're in and we wouldn't be able to keep Dad out of it."

"Then private investors," Lisa countered, feeling more than a little desperate. She may have missed out on the medical brilliance gene that Gerald had passed on to Paul, but she considered herself a decent administrator. It was the only thing about her that she felt certain her father was proud of. It was her one part in ensuring that her father's life's work lived on.

Yet she hadn't known what Derek was doing.

"We've never had investors before," Paul said.

"Pardon me for saying so, but you've never needed investors before," Ted inserted quietly. He let go of Sarah Beth's hand, which he'd been holding, and stood up. "However, it does give me an idea…"

Chapter One

Lisa stepped out of the cab and onto the sidewalk, staring at the narrow entrance of Fare, complete with uniformed doorman, ahead of her.

Why a restaurant?

Not for the first time since she'd flown from Boston to New York City was she still puzzling over the choice. Even though the meeting had been arranged by Ted Bonner, its purpose was business. Not social.

Thank heavens.

She realized the doorman was staring at her, and with a confidence that she didn't feel, smiled at the man and strode across the sidewalk, unfastening the single button on the front of her black-and-white houndstooth jacket when he ushered her into the softly lit restaurant before silently departing.

The shadowy hostess station was unattended and she waited

in the hushed silence. There was a faint strain of music, but it was subtle and nonintrusive.

Waiting to be shown to the table was okay with her. She didn't want to be there anyway. But she'd promised Paul.

She swallowed.

This is just another meeting with a potential funder.

Investor.

Her mind debated the term.

She was used to meeting with funders. Usually representatives of a philanthropic or scientific foundation to discuss research grants that the institute was seeking.

This…this was another kettle of fish, entirely. And even though it had been her idea to use investors to solve their current dilemma, she'd never in her wildest imaginings thought she'd be meeting this particular one.

She smoothed her hand over the wide belt of her high-waisted slacks and buttoned her jacket again. Switched her slender, leather briefcase from one hand to the other.

The meeting that Paul had called earlier that week replayed in her mind. She'd never seen her ever-confident, ever-capable big brother actually question whether or not the institute could survive at all and that—as much as the reason why—still had her deeply shaken.

"The gentleman is waiting for you."

Lisa blinked herself to the present where an exotically beautiful girl dressed in a narrow black sheath was smiling patiently, her hand extended slightly to one side.

She undid the button again, gripped the handle of her briefcase more tightly in her moist hand and stepped forward.

She spotted him immediately.

The "gentleman" whom Lisa would never have termed as such.

Rourke Devlin.

Billionaire venture capitalist. A man who never had to worry about finding funding for his own work because he *was* the fund. He was Ted Bonner's friend. And even though she could appreciate that fact, could appreciate the generosity he'd shown to Ted and Sara Beth during their trip to newly wedded bliss, she couldn't envision anything productive coming out of this encounter.

He was dark. Powerful. Arrogant. Rich as Midas.

And as frightening as the devil himself.

Rourke didn't even rise as she approached his small round table situated in the center of the exclusive, small restaurant. But his black gaze followed her every step of the way.

She felt like a lamb sent to slaughter and damned Derek all over again.

She might have promised Paul that she'd do her best on this meeting despite her personal reservations, but it was because of Derek that this meeting—or any of the other half dozen that she'd frenetically set up for the following week—was necessary in the first place.

A black-clothed waiter had appeared out of nowhere to pull out the second chair at the table for her.

She thanked him quietly and took her seat, tucking the briefcase on the floor next to her. There were plenty of tables surrounding them, but none was occupied. Only Rourke's, sitting here, center stage like king of the castle. "I've read reviews of Fare," she greeted him. "The food is supposed to be magnificent."

"It is."

Hardly a conversational treasure trove. She hoped it wasn't an indicator of how the rest of the meeting would go, but feared it probably was. Despite Ted's insistence that Rourke was open to meeting with her, she couldn't help but remember her encounter with him months earlier at their Founder's Ball—

and the single dance they'd shared—as well as his seeming disapproval at the time of the institute in general. "The view is lovely."

He didn't turn his head to glance at the bank of windows overlooking a pond surrounded by trees that were just now beginning to show the first hint of coming autumn. "Yes."

In her lap, her hands curled into fists beneath the protection of the white linen draping the table. All right. Forget pleasantries. She'd just get to the point. "I appreciate you meeting with me."

He lifted a sardonic eyebrow. "Do you?"

She studied him, wondering not for the first time exactly what it was about the man that seemed to place him on a different plane than others.

There were plenty of men as powerfully built. Plenty of men who possessed strikingly carved features and well-cut, thick black hair. All it took was money to buy the fine white silk shirt he wore with such casual ease. There was a single button undone at his tanned throat; a charcoal-gray suit coat discarded over the back of his chair.

He exuded confidence. Power. And he looked at her—just as he had on the other few occasions they'd been in one another's company—as if he knew things about her that she might not even know herself.

Which mostly left her feeling as if she were playing some game in which she didn't know the rules.

She moistened her lips, realizing as she did that it was an indicator of her nervousness, particularly when his gaze rested on her mouth for a moment. "I know your time is valuable."

The waiter had returned and was silently, ceremoniously presenting, then opening a bottle of wine. The cork presented and approved, the first taste mulled over, the crystal glasses partially filled. Lisa had been part of the production hundreds of times and wondered silently what any of them would say if she told them she would have preferred a fresh glass of iced tea. Wine always went straight to her head.

And it didn't take her MBA to know that she needed all of her faculties in prime working order when it came to dealing with Rourke Devlin, who hadn't volunteered even a polite disclaimer about the value of his time.

But she said nothing. Merely smiled and picked up the glass, sipping at the crisp, cool Chardonnay. It *was* delicious. Something she might have chosen for herself if she were in the mood for wine. But she would have pegged Rourke as a red wine sort of man. To go along with the raw red meat those strong white teeth could probably tear apart.

"I told the chef we'd have his recommendation," Rourke said. "Raoul never disappoints."

"How nice." She really, *really* wished they were meeting in his office. This just seemed far too intimate. Additional diners around them would have helped dispel that impression. "Isn't Fare usually open for lunch?" It was well past noon. And the reviews she'd read about the place had indicated it took months to get a reservation.

"Usually."

Which explained *so* much. She lifted the wineglass again and thought she saw the faintest glimmer of amusement hovering around his mobile lips. And it suddenly dawned on her why they were in a restaurant and not his office.

Because he'd known it would set her on edge.

She wasn't sure why that certainty was so suddenly clear. But it was. She knew it right down in her bones. And the glint in his eyes as he watched her while he lifted his own wineglass seemed to confirm it.

She set down her glass and reached down to pull a narrow file out of her briefcase. "Ted gave you some indication why we wanted to meet with you." It wasn't a question. She knew that Ted Bonner had primed the pump, so to speak, with his old buddy, when he'd arranged the meeting once Paul had jumped on the bandwagon of approval. "This prospectus will outline the advantages and opportunities of investing in the Armstrong Fertility Institute." She started to hand the file over to Rourke, only to stop midway, when he lifted a few fingers, as if to wave off the presentation that they'd pulled together at the institute in record time.

Not that he could know that.

Ted wouldn't have told the man just how desperate things had become. Friendship or not, Dr. Bonner was now a firmly entrenched part of the Armstrong Institute team. And *nobody* on that team wanted word to get out about the reason underlying their unusual foray into seeking investors. Their reputation would never recover. Not after the string of bad press they'd already endured. Their patients wouldn't want their names—some very well-known—associated with the institute. And without patients, there wouldn't just be layoffs. The institute would simply have to close its doors.

Damn you, Derek.

She lowered the prospectus and set it on the linen cloth next to the fancy little bread basket that the waiter delivered, along with a selection of spreads.

"Put it away," Rourke said. "I prefer not to discuss business while I'm eating."

"Then why didn't you schedule me for when you weren't?" The question popped out and she wanted to kick herself. Instead, she lifted her chin a little and made herself meet his gaze, pretending as if she weren't riddled with frustration.

He was toying with her. She didn't have the slightest clue as to why he would even bother.

And she also left the folder right where it was. A glossy

reminder of why they were meeting, even if he was determined to avoid it.

He pulled the wine bottle from the sterling ice bucket standing next to the table and refilled her glass even though she'd only consumed a small amount. "Have a roll," he said. "Raoul's wife, Gina, makes them fresh every day."

"I don't eat much bread," she said bluntly. What was the point of pretending congeniality? "Are you interested in discussing an investment in the institute or not?" If he wasn't—which was what she'd *tried* to tell Paul and the others—then she was wasting her time that would be better spent in preparation for meeting with investors who were.

"More bread would look good on you," he said. His gaze traveled over her, seeming to pick apart everything from the customary chignon in her hair to the single silver ring she wore on her right thumb. "You've lost weight since I last saw you."

There was no way to mistake the accusation as a compliment and her lips parted. She stared, letting the offense ripple through her until she could settle it somewhere out of the way. "Women can never be too thin," she reminded him coolly, and picked up the wineglass again. Might as well partake of the excellent vintage since it was apparent that he wasn't taking their meeting seriously, anyway.

No doubt he'd agreed simply to get Ted off his back.

"A ridiculous assumption made by women for women," Rourke returned. "Most men prefer curves and softness against them over jutting bones."

"Well." She swallowed more wine. "That's something you and I won't have to worry about."

He looked amused again and turned his head, glancing at the bank of windows. His profile was sharp, as defined—and cold—as a chiseled piece of granite. His black hair sprang sharply away from his forehead and the fine crow's-feet arrowing out from the corner of his eyes were clearly illuminated.

Unfortunately, they didn't detract from the total package.

"The view here *is* good," he said. "I'm glad Raoul went with my suggestion on the location. Initially he was looking for a high-rise."

She wanted to grind her teeth together, as annoyed with her own distraction where Rourke-the-man was concerned as she was with his unpredictability. "I didn't know that restaurants were something you invested in. Techno-firm startups seemed to be more your speed. Aren't restaurants notoriously chancy?" She lifted a hand, silently indicating the empty tables around them.

"Venture capitalism is about taking chances." He selected a roll from the basket and broke it open, slathering one of the compound butters over half. "Calculated chances, of course. But as it happens, in the five years since Raoul opened the doors, I've never had cause to regret this particular chance." He held out the roll. "Taste it."

She could feel the wine wending its heady way through her veins. Breakfast had been hours ago. Wait. She'd skipped breakfast, in favor of a conference call.

Which meant drinking even the tiniest amount of wine was more foolish than usual.

Arguing seemed too much work, though, so she took the roll from him. Their fingers brushed.

She shoved the bread in her mouth, chomping down on it as viciously as she chomped down on the warmth that zipped through her hand.

"Good?"

Chewing, she nodded. The roll *was* good. Deliciously so. It only annoyed her more.

She chased the yeasty heaven down with more wine and

leaned closer to the table. "Obviously excellent bread and wine isn't always enough to ensure success, or this place *would* be busting at the seams."

"Raoul closed Fare until dinner for me."

She blinked slowly and sat back. "Why?"

"Because I asked him to."

"Again…why?"

"Because I wanted to be alone with you."

A puff of air escaped her lips. "But you don't even like me."

Rourke picked up his wineglass and studied the disbelieving expression of the woman across from him. "Maybe not," he allowed.

Lisa Armstrong had looked like an ice princess the first time he'd seen her more than six months ago in a crowded Cambridge pub called Shots where he'd been meeting with Ted Bonner and Chance Demetrios.

He'd had no reason to change his opinion in the few times he'd seen her since.

"But I want you," he continued smoothly, watching the sudden flare of her milk-chocolate eyes. "And you want me." He'd known that since he'd maneuvered her into sharing a single, brief dance with him months earlier.

Her lips had parted. They were slightly thin, slightly wide for her narrow, angular face, and a shade of pale, delicate pink that he figured owed nothing to cosmetics.

And he hadn't been able to get them out of his mind.

Obviously recovering, those lips pursed slightly. Her eyebrows—darker than the gold that covered her head—returned to their usual, level places. Her brown gaze was only fractionally less sharp than it had been when she'd first sat down across from him. But a strand of hair had worked loose of that perfect, smooth knot at the nape of her neck and had curled around her slender neck to tease the hollow at the base of her throat. "You have an incredible ego, Mr. Devlin."

So he'd been told. By foes, friends and family alike. He pulled his gaze from that single, loose lock of hair that tickled the visible pulse he could see beneath her fair, fair skin. "I don't think it's egotism to recognize facts. And you might as well make it Rourke."

"Why?" She didn't seem to realize she'd reached for the other half of the roll he'd buttered and flicked a glance at it before dropping it back on the small bread plate. "Are we going to be doing business together after all?"

His inclination was to admit that they weren't.

But he also had plenty of good reasons to want to ensure that Ted Bonner and Chance Demetrios were able to continue their work without any more hitches. Investing in anything that Ted was involved in would be a good bet.

But through the Armstrong Fertility Institute?

Not even Ted knew why that particular idea was anathema to him.

Maybe it was small of him, but he wasn't ready yet to release Lisa Armstrong from this particular hook. He was enjoying, too much, having the ice princess right where he wanted her.

He hid a dark bolt of amusement directed squarely at himself.

Nearly where he wanted her.

"Our salads," he said instead, glancing at Tonio, their waiter and Raoul's youngest son, as he approached with his tray.

He could see the ire creep back into Lisa's eyes.

She controlled it well, though. Merely smiling coolly at Rourke as Tonio served them. He wondered if beneath that facade she would have preferred giving him a swift kick or if she really was that cool, all the way through.

It would be interesting to find out.

Interesting but complicated as hell.

He picked up his fork, his appetite whetted on more levels than he presently cared to admit. "Eat," he said when she looked as if she weren't even going to taste Raoul's concoction. He hadn't been exaggerating when he'd observed that she'd lost weight.

At the Founder's Ball in her floaty gown of slippery brown and white that had hugged her narrow hips and left the entirety of her ivory back and shoulders distractingly bare, she'd felt slender and delicate in his arms.

Now, even with the thick weave of her jacket and the wide-cut legs of her slacks, he could tell she was even thinner.

She took her work to heart.

He could have told that for himself, even if Ted hadn't mentioned it.

Often in the office before anyone else arrived. Often there later than anyone stayed.

For Ted to even *notice* something like that, beyond his Bunsen burners and beakers, was something. He'd said she was a workaholic.

Ironically, that gave her and Rourke something in common.

She was poking at the tomato salad and he was glad to see that some of it actually reached her mouth. His sister Tricia would take one look at her and want to fatten her up with plenty of pasta.

"How long have you and Dr. Bonner been friends?"

He had to give her points for adaptability. He'd expected to receive a mostly chilly silence for his autocratic refusal to discuss what they both knew she'd traveled to New York City to discuss. "Since we were boys."

Her gaze flicked over him. "I find it hard to envision you as a boy. Were you schoolmates?"

He almost laughed.

Ted Bonner had grown up with wealth and privilege. Rourke and his three sisters might have had the same, if their father hadn't walked out on them when they were young. Instead, the Devlin clan had gone from being comfortable to being…not.

They'd been locked out of their fine Boston home with no ceremony, no explanations.

He'd been twelve years old.

For a while, his mother had struggled to keep them in Boston. He and his sisters had switched from private to public schools. They'd moved into a basement apartment a lifestyle away from what they'd been used to. But in the end, within a handful of years, Nina Devlin had simply been forced to move them all back to New York where they'd moved into the cramped apartment above the home-style Italian restaurant his grandparents owned and operated.

And Rourke's father? He'd landed in California with a surgically enhanced trophy wife who'd been fewer than ten years older than Rourke.

He'd seen them only once. When he'd been twenty-three and had raked in a cool million over his first real deal.

That was when Trophy Wife had indicated a considerable interest in Rourke's bed and Dad had claimed Rourke was a chip off the old block.

He'd never seen either one of them again.

"Ted and I were in the same Boy Scout troop," he told Lisa, fully expecting the surprise she couldn't hide. Before they'd left Boston, his mother had chugged him across town to keep him involved in the troop that he'd been drafted into by his father, before he'd skipped. Rourke had hated it until he and Ted had struck up an unlikely friendship.

"*You* were a Boy Scout."

"Trustworthy, loyal, helpful, friendly—" He broke off the litany of Scout law when she snorted softly.

"Sorry," she said, but aside from the bloom of pink over her sharp cheekbones, she didn't particularly look it. "I just have a whole mental image of you wearing khaki shorts and merit badges." The tip of her tongue appeared between her pearl-white teeth. Then she laughed softly, and shook her head. "A considerable change from your usual attire."

He dragged his gaze away from the humorous stretch of her lips only to get caught in the sparkle of her eyes.

He tamped down on the heat shooting through him.

He hadn't seen her smile, really smile, since that first glimpse of her at Shots when she'd been laughing over something with her friend Sara Beth.

Glancing at Tonio, who immediately cleared away their salads, Rourke picked up the prospectus. "The Armstrong Institute's been plagued with bad press," he said, breaking his own trumped-up rule of no business over lunch. "Questionable research protocols. Padded statistics."

"Both allegations were proved false. By none other than your Scout buddy, Ted."

"Yet the bad aftertaste of innuendo remains."

The sparkle in her eyes died, leaving her expression looking hauntingly hollow. "That's a little like blaming the victim, isn't it? The Armstrong Institute has never operated with anything less than integrity. Nor has any of its staff. But we're to be held accountable now for someone else's shoddy reporting?"

"Integrity." He mulled the word over, watching her while Tonio returned again with their main course of lobster risotto. "Interesting choice of words."

Her gaze didn't waver as she reached for her wineglass again. "I cannot imagine why."

She would be a good poker player, he decided. Not everyone could baldly lie like that without so much as a blink. She was even better at it than his ex-wife had been.

But for the moment, he let the matter drop. "Eat the risotto. It's nearly as good as my mother's."

She picked up her fork and took a small bite. Poked at the risotto as if moving the creamy rice around her plate would be an adequate substitute for actually eating. "Investment in the Armstrong Fertility Institute would be along the line of similar projects for Devlin Ventures. You've had great success in medically related firms."

"None of which was family controlled," he said flatly. "I don't do family-owned businesses."

"You invested in Fare."

"I'm a *partner* in Fare."

Lisa's gaze finally fell, but not quickly enough to hide the defeat that filled it. She set down the fork with care. Dabbed the corner of her lips with her linen napkin before laying it on the table. "I believe I've wasted enough of your time. Clearly you agreed to this meeting only because of your friendship with Ted." She pushed her chair back a few inches and picked up her briefcase as she rose. Her gaze flicked back to him for a moment. "Please assure Raoul that my departure is no reflection on his excellent meal."

She turned away and started to leave the dining room.

"I'm surprised you would give up so quickly," he said. "So easily. I would have thought you were all about duty to the institute."

He saw her shoulders stiffen beneath the stylish jacket. She slowly turned, clasping the handle of her briefcase in both hands in front of her. "I am. And that duty dictates that my time is better served on prospective investors. Not dallying over amazing risotto and good wine with a man who has a different agenda. Whatever that may be."

He had no agenda where the institute was concerned. With the single exception of his unwelcome attraction to *her*, anything to do with the Armstrong family put a vile taste in his mouth.

"The institute is on the brink of financial collapse," he said evenly. "I'm not in the habit of throwing away good money."

"The institute is experiencing some financial hiccups," she returned coolly. "Nothing from which we cannot recover. And if you didn't have some burr under your saddle that I still fail to understand, you'd be able to recognize that fact, too."

"That's what you really believe." It was almost incomprehensible. The losses that the institute had incurred were nearly insurmountable.

Her chin angled slightly.

Too thin. Too tense.

But undeniably beautiful and certainly dutiful to her cause.

"Fine. We'll meet in the morning."

She lifted an eyebrow. "Where? Your favorite breakfast shop?"

He very nearly smiled. The ice princess did have a claw or two. "My office. Nine o'clock."

Her eyebrow lowered. Her eyes flared for a moment. She nodded. "Very well."

"And don't be late. I'll be squeezing you into the day as it is."

"I'm never late," she assured him and, with a small smile, turned on her heel and strode out.

He watched her go, waiting to see if she'd glance back.

She did. But not until she was nearly out of sight. He still managed to hold her gaze for a second longer than was comfortable.

Her cheeks filled with color. This time when she turned to go, there was a lot more *run* in her stride.

How far would duty take her?

He picked up his wine, smiling faintly. It would be interesting finding out.

Chapter Two

"Of *course* he's going to invest." Sara Beth Bonner's voice was bright and confident through the cell phone's speaker. "Why else would he ask you to come to his office this morning?"

"I don't know." Lisa shook her head, glancing from the phone that was sitting on the vanity in her hotel room, to her reflection in the mirror. She'd already smudged her mascara once and had had to start over. She didn't have time to mess up again, or—despite her falsely confident assurance to Rourke the day before—she would be late for their appointment that morning. "I know he's an old friend of your brand-new husband, but the man's a player. I don't *know* what he wants."

"Ted keeps saying Rourke is rock-solid."

Lisa made a face at her reflection. The man *was* rock-solid—she'd found that out for herself when they'd danced together at the Founder's Ball. But that, of course, wasn't what

Ted meant. "Just because Rourke was Boy Scout material once, doesn't mean he still is."

"What does Paul say?"

Lisa decided her mascara was finally acceptable and closed the tube with one hand while reaching for her lipstick with the other. "The same thing. That of course I can convince Devlin to jump on board." She smoothed the subtle pink onto her lips. "Unfortunately, Paul doesn't seem to grasp the fact that such blind faith only makes the pressure worse."

"It's not blind faith," Sara Beth assured her. "It's confidence. Come on, Lisa. Don't start doubting yourself now. You can do this."

"When did you trade in your nurse's uniform for a cheerleader's?"

"Hmm." Laughter filled Sara Beth's voice. "I wonder how Ted would feel about me in a short little skirt, waving pompoms around."

Lisa groaned. "Newlyweds," she returned. "Listen, I've gotta run. My flight gets in around three so I'll probably see you at the institute before you get off. Shift, I mean."

"Nice."

"What are friends for?" She disconnected the phone, but she was finally smiling.

Thank goodness for Sara Beth. Her friend never failed to cheer her up.

She smoothed her hand once more over her pulled-back hair and pushed the phone into the pocket of her briefcase. She hadn't come to New York the day before prepared for an overnight, which had necessitated a quick trip out to find something suitable to wear for today's meeting because she refused to meet with Rourke again looking like day-old bread.

Since she'd already spent a small fortune on her Armani ensemble for the debacle of the day before, her personal budget was definitely taking a hit. But the black skirt she wore with the same black jersey tee from yesterday looked crisp and suitably "don't mess with me" teamed with the new taupe blazer. She looked good and wasn't going to pretend that it didn't help bolster her confidence where the man was concerned.

She pushed her bare feet into her high-heeled black pumps, snatched up the briefcase and hurried out the door.

The morning air was brisk and breezy, tugging both at her chignon and her skirt as she waited for the cab that the doorman hailed for her.

The traffic was heavy—no surprise—and she wished that she hadn't taken time to phone her mother that morning. It would have been one less item taking up time, and it wasn't as if Emily Stanton Armstrong had had anything helpful or productive to say, anyway.

The only thing that Lisa had in common with her mother was a devotion to the man they had in common—Gerald. The great "Dr. G." She'd given up, years ago, trying to understand what made her mother tick, much less trying to gain her approval. Emily already had the perfect daughter in Olivia, anyway. Olivia was the wife of a senator, for heaven's sake. Jamison Mallory was the youngest member of the U.S. Senate and the eldest son of Boston's most powerful family. He might as well be royalty. And he was probably headed for the White House. Olivia and Jamison had even recently adopted two children who'd lost their own parents, completing their picture of the perfect family. Rarely did a week pass when Lisa's sister and brother-in-law weren't featured in either the society section or the national news.

Not that Lisa was jealous of her older sister. Olivia looked better—happier—now than she had in years. Lisa just never felt as if they were quite on the same page. The things they wanted in life had always been so different.

She sighed a little, brushing her hands nervously over her skirt. She *had* to pull the institute out of the fire.

The cab finally pulled up in front of the towering building that housed Devlin Ventures. A glance at her chunky bangle watch told her she had nearly ten minutes to spare.

Perfect.

She quickly paid and tipped the driver and left the cab, weaving between the pedestrians on the sidewalk to enter the building. Gleaming marble, soaring windows, shops and an atrium filled with live trees greeted her. It was impressive, and if she'd had more time, she probably would have wandered around the first floor, just to explore. But since she didn't, she aimed for the information desk that ran the length of one wall.

In minutes, she possessed a visitor's pass that got her through the security door that wasn't even visible from where she'd entered, and had bulleted dizzyingly to the top floor of the building in an elevator that went strictly to that floor, and that floor alone.

Devlin Ventures wasn't merely an occupant of the building.

It was the owner.

She barely had time to smooth her hand over her hair and run her tongue discreetly over her teeth to remove any misplaced lipstick before the elevator doors opened and she stepped out onto a floor that was as calm and soothing as the first floor had been busy and vibrant.

For some reason, she hadn't envisioned Rourke Devlin as a man to surround himself with such a Zen-like environment.

A curving desk in pale wood that matched the floor faced the elevator and she stopped in front of it. "Good morning," she told the girl sitting there. "I'm Lisa Armstrong. I have an appointment with Mr. Devlin."

The model-thin girl consulted something behind her desk, and seemed to find what she was looking for. "I'll show you to his office." She rose and swayed her way along a wide corridor. At the end, she turned, hip jutted, and lifted a languid hand. "Cynthia is Mr. Devlin's assistant," she said. "She'll see to you now."

Lisa found herself facing a woman who was as unattractive as the receptionist was attractive, right down to the heavy black-framed glasses that did little to disguise a hawkish nose. "Good morning."

Rourke's assistant gave her a short glance. "Mr. Devlin is unavoidably detained. I'm afraid he can't see you as scheduled."

Lisa felt her chest tighten. Dismay. Annoyance. Disappointment. They all clogged her system, jockeying for first place. "I'm happy to wait," she assured her.

Cynthia gave her an unemotional stare that told her absolutely nothing. "If you wish." Her gaze drifted to the collection of low, brown leather chairs situated near the windows.

Taking the cue, Lisa headed toward them. The view would have been spectacular if she had been in the mood to appreciate it.

Would Rourke stoop to blowing her off like this, without so much as meeting her face-to-face?

It didn't seem to fit, but what did she know?

The man was impossibly unpredictable.

She set her briefcase on the floor beside one of the chairs that had a view of the important one—the entrance, so she wouldn't miss spotting Rourke when he came in. If he came in.

The minutes dragged by and she tried not to fidget. She was used to being *busy,* not cooling her heels like this. But she sat. And she waited and she watched.

Several people came and went. She honestly couldn't tell whether they were members of Rourke's staff or visitors. Cynthia of the ugly glasses seemed to treat them all in the same way.

Nobody came to sit in one of the other chairs near Lisa,

though. And after at least an hour of sitting there, she pulled out her BlackBerry. Answered a few dozen e-mails. Listened to even more voice mail messages. Her secretary, Ella, confirmed that she'd successfully rescheduled the appointments that she'd originally had on her calendar for that day.

The last message was from Derek.

As soon as she heard her brother's voice, her teeth felt on edge. She skipped the message, neither listening to it, nor deleting it.

Her fingers tightened around the phone and she turned to stare out the windows.

How could her brother have *stolen* from the institute—from his own family—the way he had?

How could she not have realized? Suspected?

She should have just deleted the message. There was nothing Derek could have to say that she wanted to hear.

Not now.

Unfortunately, beneath the anger that bolstered her was a horrible, pained void that she couldn't quite pretend didn't exist.

"You waited."

She jerked her head around to see Rourke standing less than a foot away. The phone slipped out of her hand, landing on the ivory-colored rug that sat beneath the arrangement of chairs. "We had an appointment." Her voice was appallingly thick and she leaned forward quickly to retrieve her phone.

He beat her to it, though, and she froze, still leaning forward, her face disconcertingly close to his as he crouched there.

He slowly set the phone in her outstretched palm, but didn't release it even when her fingers closed around it. His dark, dark gaze roved over her face.

She felt almost as if he'd stroked his fingers along her temple. Her cheek. Her jaw.

"What's wrong?" His voice was low. As soft as that never-there touch.

Everything.

The word nearly slipped out and, realizing it, she quickly straightened. The phone slid free of his grasp; once again hers alone. She tucked it into her briefcase. "Other than enjoying the view for the past two hours? Not a thing."

His expression hardened a little, making her realize—belatedly—that it had been softer after all. For a moment. Only a moment.

He straightened. "You should have rescheduled."

Cynthia was at her desk, but that was a good thirty feet away. Still, Lisa kept her voice low. "And waste another morning?"

"For someone courting my financing, you're sounding very waspish."

The damnable thing was, he was right. And if he were anyone else, she would have sat there all day, happily, and still had a smile on her face when he finally got around to meeting with her.

"I'm sorry." She rose. "It's not you." Not entirely, anyway. "And of course, if you would like me to reschedule, I'll do so."

He studied her for a moment. "I have to make a small trip today."

Even prepared for it, she felt buffeted by more dismay.

But before she could formulate a suitable reply, he'd leaned over and picked up her briefcase. "Come on."

He was heading for the elevator, not even stopping to speak to Cynthia along the way. Lisa had to skip to catch up with him and stepped onto the elevator when he held it open for her. "You don't have to escort me from the building to make sure I leave," she said when the doors closed on them. He held the briefcase away from her when she snatched at it.

"I'm sure you learned somewhere along the way that you get more flies with honey," he observed.

"Fly strips work amazingly well, too," she countered and folded her hands together. She was *not* going to play tug-of-war with the man where her own briefcase was concerned.

His lips twitched.

For some reason the descending elevator seemed to creep along, in direct contrast to the way it seemed to have shot her to his floor when she'd arrived. He turned and faced her, leaning back against the wall that was paneled in gleaming mahogany with narrow mirrored inserts. "You look nice today."

Her lips parted. She blinked and looked up at the digital floor display above the door. Thirty. Twenty-nine. Twenty-eight. "Thank you." He looked nice today, too. Mouth-watering nice.

Which was a direction her thoughts didn't need to take.

"Did you sleep well?"

Even more disconcerted, she slid him a quick glance, then looked back up at the display. "Yes, thank you. My hotel was comfortable." It was hardly The Plaza, but then she was on an expense account. Unlike her wardrobe, the cash-strapped institute would foot the bill for this little junket. As such, the room was moderately priced and not entirely conveniently located. She glanced at her watch. "My flight leaves this afternoon."

Twenty-four. Twenty-three.

"Do you ever wear your hair down?"

"I beg your pardon?"

He pushed his hand in his trousers pocket, dislodging the excellent lay of his black suit coat. "It's long, isn't it?"

Eighteen. Seventeen.

"A bit," she allowed, trying to figure out what angle he was coming from.

"I've never seen you wear it down."

She huffed a little, exasperated not just with him, but with the eternal slowness of the elevator. "Since you've seen me only a handful of times, is that so surprising?" She didn't like—or trust—the faint smile hovering around his lips. "If we're going to be asking for personal information, then what was it that had you—" her voice dropped into a toneless imitation of Cynthia's "—unavoidably detained?" She raised her eyebrows expectantly.

"My mother was in the hospital last night."

Stricken, her eyebrows lowered. "Oh. I'm sorry." She looked more closely at him. He didn't look unduly upset. His suit was as magazine-perfect as always, his eyes clear and sharp; he didn't look as if he'd spent the night in some hospital waiting room. "She's all right?"

"A sprained ankle that they thought might be broken."

"Oh. That's good then. Well. Not good that she has a sprain, of course. But—" She realized she was babbling and broke off.

Fortunately, the elevator finally rocked softly to a stop and the doors slid open. He waited for her to exit first but he still held her briefcase. And continued to do so, either oblivious to, or choosing to ignore, her awkward gestures of taking it back.

They were nearly to the main entrance and he was still in possession of it when he spoke again. "Your security pass."

She'd completely forgotten it. She unclipped it from her lapel and dropped it off at the desk, then rejoined Rourke where he was waiting. "I didn't realize you owned the building," she said, holding out her hand for what seemed the tenth time. "It's quite an impressive space."

He glanced around. "It'll do." Then he took her hand, as if that was what she'd been waiting for, and tugged her through the doors.

Feeling as if she'd dropped through the looking glass, she couldn't do anything but follow.

Outside, the breeze had picked up, but the sun had warmed,

foretelling a perfectly lovely September day. She caught her skirt with her free hand before it could blow up around her knees. "I'll contact your assistant to reschedule."

"No need. Come with me." He released her hand, and touched the small of her back, directing her inexorably toward a black limo that was parked at the curb.

She tried digging in her heels, but that was about as effective as holding down her skirt against the mischievous breeze, and before she knew it, she was ensconced in the rear of the spacious limousine.

With him.

And what *should* have felt spacious…didn't. Not when his thigh was only six inches away from hers and she could smell the heady scent of him. Fresh. Clean. A little spicy.

"Mr. Devlin—"

"Rourke."

A jolt of nervous excitement whisked through her. Maybe all wasn't lost, after all.

On the other hand, maybe he was merely planning to drop her at her hotel.

The teeter-totter of possibilities was enough to make her dizzy and answers were the only thing that would solve that. So she obliged him. "Rourke." Warmth bloomed in her cheeks at the feel of his name on her lips. "Where are you taking me?"

"Greenwich."

"*What?* Why?" It would surely take an hour each way, and that was if the traffic didn't get heavier.

But he just lifted his hand, putting her off as he put his vibrating cell phone to his ear.

She fell silent and sank deeper into the butter-soft leather seat, crossing her arms and kissing goodbye any chance she had of making her flight home on time.

He was still talking, so she reached for her briefcase—at

last—and pulled out her own phone, sending a quick message to Ella that she'd need to move back her flight. Again.

Then, leaving that to her trusty assistant, she scrolled through her e-mails—two from Derek which she ignored as surely as she'd ignored his voice mail—and then dropped the phone back into her briefcase in favor of looking out the window.

She was even beyond trying to puzzle out what Rourke was up to, because she just ended up with a headache, anyway.

He stayed on the phone the entire drive—his voice low and steady as he discussed some upcoming media launch—and she found herself struggling against drowsiness. When the car finally turned up a long, winding drive bordered by immaculate lawns and massive shrubs, some still blooming, Rourke finally put away his phone.

They passed an island of tall, slender cypress trees bordering a flowing fountain, then a terraced swimming pool, and after rounding yet another curve in the drive, came to a stop in front of an immense Tudor mansion.

"It's beautiful." She couldn't stop the exclamation when they stepped out of the car. "Who lives here?"

"My mom." He didn't head toward the grand entrance, fronted by a dozen wide, shallow stone steps, but instead to a smaller, more unobtrusive door well off to one side.

She hurried after him, her heels clacking against the pavement.

He stopped and waited until she caught up to him, and they went in through the door. "You grew up here?" Her voice echoed a little in the long, empty hall they found themselves in.

"Hell, no." He reached back and grabbed her hand unerringly—sending a shuddering quake through her that she tried to ignore—then turned and left through another door that led outside onto a stone terrace.

She immediately heard the high-pitched squeal of children's laughter and Rourke let go of her hand just in time to catch up the little girl who aimed for him with the speed and accuracy of a heat-seeking missile.

It was all Lisa could do not to gape as his face broke into a full-blown smile while he swung the blond-haired imp up in the air, earning another peal of squealing laughter from her. She caught his face between her starfish fingers and pressed a smacking kiss against his lips. "What'd you bring me?"

Rourke laughed outright and hitched the little girl on his shoulder, tickling her knees beneath the short hem of her miniature white tennis dress. "This," he told Lisa, "greedy little one is my youngest niece, Tanya. Say hello to Ms. Armstrong, munchkin."

"Is she your girlfriend?"

Lisa nearly choked, particularly when Rourke sent her a sidelong look. "Does she *look* like she's my girlfriend?"

The little girl's eyes were just as dark as Rourke's; a startling contrast considering the golden curls spilling around her head. And they focused on Lisa with an unnerving intensity. "Maybe," she determined. "But I'm gonna marry Uncle Rourke, anyway. He's mine."

Lisa couldn't help but smile. "I see."

"I'm five, so I gotta wait a while. But you can still play with him," Tanya said generously. Her hand patted Rourke's head as if he was a particularly good pet. "I'm not very good yet." She pointed toward the tennis court on the far side of yet another swimming pool. There were a half-dozen kids trotting around the court, batting tennis balls back and forth more like ammunition than in any semblance of a real tennis match.

Trying not to blush—because the second Tanya had said *play,* her uncle had given Lisa a look that left her feeling scorched—she caught at her blowing skirt again and focused anywhere other than on Rourke. "Are those your brothers and sisters?" She nodded toward the other children.

"They're my cousins. I'm a lonely only," Tanya said so pathetically that Lisa had to bite back a laugh.

"Lonely my foot," Rourke chided, lifting her off his shoulder and flipping her heels over head before setting her on her feet. "Where's your grandma?"

"Aunt Tricia said she hadda sit in the shade with her foot elevatored." She gestured toward the lagoon-shaped swimming pool where several lounges and chairs were arranged around tables shaded by large beige market umbrellas. If it weren't for the thick border of trees well off in the distance that were showing faint shades of fall, it would have seemed like the middle of summer.

"Run ahead and tell her I'm here with a guest."

Tanya immediately turned on her little sneakered feet and raced across the stone courtyard, dashing down the terraced steps and across the lawn toward the pool.

Lisa caught at her drifting skirt again. A rerun of her trousers from the day before would have been smarter. "Rourke, you could have just said you wanted to check on your mother. I would have understood the need to reschedule our meeting." If anything, his evident concern for his mother made him seem much more human than she'd previously suspected.

"Rescheduling isn't necessary."

The teeter-totter was back in full force. "Because…?" She trailed off warily.

"Because I already know what I need to know." He lifted his hand in a wave when a petite woman appeared from beneath one of the umbrellas and started toward them. "That's Tricia. Be prepared. She likes bossing everyone around."

Her jaw tightened. He was being deliberately obscure. "Runs in the family, evidently," she murmured.

But he just grabbed her wrist and strode off again, pulling her with him whether she wanted to go or not and not releasing her until he met his dark-haired sister and swept her into an unrestrained hug that surprised Lisa all over again.

Then he held out his arm toward Lisa, introducing them. "This is my sister Tricia McAllister. Trish, this is Lisa Armstrong."

Feeling awkward, Lisa stuck out her hand. "It's nice to meet you."

Tricia had the same scrutinizing black eyes her brother possessed and they were clearly speculative as she looked from Lisa to Rourke and back again. "And you," she returned, exchanging a quick handshake before addressing her brother again. "Cara and Lea are bringing lunch down any minute now. It's so lovely out, I said we had to eat outside. So come say hello to Mother and then pull two more chairs over to her table." She headed off.

Rourke caught Lisa's eye. "See?"

"Is she the oldest?"

"Of my sisters, yes."

Which, she assumed, meant he was older than they were. "Brothers?"

He shook his had. "Until Trish had her third kid—Trey—I was the only guy in the group, save a couple of brothers-in-law." He wrapped his hand around her elbow, steering her toward the tables beyond which the pool shimmered like pale clouds floating in liquid silver. "Now smile and stop looking like you're heading to your own execution."

"I'm sorry. But I feel like I'm intruding here."

"It's just family."

"Right. Your family." The back of her neck itched. "I'm here on business but they probably think this is social." At least that was what the speculation on Tricia's face had indicated.

He lifted an eyebrow. "So?"

"So—" She broke off, her hands flapping uselessly. She'd left the briefcase—along with her means of contact with the outside world—in the limo. And with each step they took, her heels sinking into the still-lush lawn, she felt as if she was getting further away from that familiar world in favor of this resortlike home. "It's…it's not."

"You'll have your money. All of it. Now relax." Completely disregarding the shock that had her legs nearly going out beneath her, his steps didn't hesitate as he continued pulling her toward the others. "Think of us as one happy family."

Chapter Three

All of it?

Lisa barely heard anything after those three little words. She supposed she must have functioned through the meal—carried from the house by Cara and Lea, who turned out to be Rourke's other sisters. Rourke sat her across from his mother, Nina. She had one bandaged foot elevated on a second chair, a position that didn't prevent her from busily working the colorful blanket she was crocheting. Like a general maneuvering her troops, Tricia called in all the children from the tennis courts, directing them around the two other tables even as she tossed out introductions that Lisa had no hope of following.

Not when *all of it* kept circling in her head, even trumping that ironic "happy family" comment.

He couldn't have meant it literally. Could he?

Before she knew it, the meal was done, the oddly prosaic plastic plates and utensils disposed of and after being indulgently waved off by Nina Devlin, Lisa found herself walking through an honest-to-goodness hedge maze with Rourke while three of his nieces—Tanya in the lead—raced ahead of them.

"What exactly do you mean by *all of it?*" she finally asked.

They'd both left behind their jackets at the table. He'd rolled the cuffs of his white shirt up his forearms. Even his tie was gone. And at her abrupt question, he stopped and looked at her. The hedge was tall enough that it couldn't be seen over, but not so high that it felt claustrophobic. She could hear the high-pitched little-girl voices ahead of them, and still feel the breeze tugging at her chignon and her skirt.

But when he focused his attention on her face just then, they might as well have been locked together, alone, in a four-by-four vault. "I mean *all of it,*" he repeated as if she were witless.

Which was pretty much how she felt. Ultimately, the institute needed millions, and the most practical solution—if the least desirable—to that would have been from multiple sources. Not even Ted had really believed that Rourke would consider covering their entire need. "But—"

He lifted a hand, silencing her. "This isn't up for discussion. I'm willing to invest as much as it takes, but I'll be the only investor. No others."

Her blood was zipping through her veins more quickly, excitement making her pulse pound. This was it, then. Truly it.

The answer to a prayer.

"Are you agreeing because of your friendship with Ted?"

"Does it matter?"

She slowly shook her head. "What matters is the institute."

"Right." His lips twisted a little. "As it happens, I do want to see Ted and Chance have every opportunity available to them. And Ted won't leave the institute."

Her shoes crunched on the smooth gravel of the path as she took two steps one way, then back again. "You asked him?"

His eyes glinted, reminding her needlessly that—indulgent uncle or not—he was a calculating businessman. "Of course."

She swallowed. Paul had courted Ted and Chance away from San Francisco. With the institute in its currently precarious position, could she blame them if they were courted away from *them?*

"Ted flatly refused, though," Rourke added. "Wouldn't even consider any of the institutions I brought to his attention. Which is good. Because without Bonner and Demetrios I wouldn't touch this with a ten-foot pole." His eyes narrowed. "I know the numbers, Lisa. More importantly, I know why."

He couldn't possibly know that Derek was the cause. But she knew that before the *t*'s were crossed and the *i*'s dotted, he'd have a right to know the truth. For now, though, she chose to skirt it. "With such a level of financial commitment, are you expecting to be more hands-on in a functional capacity?"

He looked darkly amused. "Afraid I'm going to want to set up an office next to yours?" They turned another corner of the maze.

"Of course not," she blithely lied. The Armstrongs ran the Armstrong Fertility Institute. If she had anything to say about it, that was the way it would continue. "Naturally, you'll want some assurance that your investment is protected, so I—"

"It'll be protected all right. Just not by my regular presence during your management meetings. I'm not interested in telling you what staff to hire and fire or what sort of patient load every physician should maintain or what research protocols should be followed. The institute already knows all that."

Given the grim set of his mouth, she wasn't certain if there was a compliment in there or not.

She was leaning toward *not.*

"Then what, exactly, *do* you mean by protection?" The institute had been in successful operation for more than two decades. With the exception of their run of bad press during the past year, the only instance of mismanagement was what they were dealing with now.

Of course that instance was a freaking whopper.

"I mean *you*."

She frowned, trying—and failing—to decipher his meaning. "I have no intention of deserting the institute," she assured him. She'd had plenty of offers in the past few years, offers she'd never taken seriously, because her heart was in Cambridge, firmly entrenched in her family's calling. "I'll be there as long as there's a lightbulb burning."

He shrugged. "That's up to you."

Which left her more confused than ever. But a clatter of gravel heralded the giggling trio as the girls ran past them on their way back out of the maze and Lisa waited until they were gone again before speaking. "We're talking in circles, Rourke."

But he didn't answer immediately.

Instead, he closed his hand over her elbow and led her around another corner.

They'd reached the center of the maze where four short benches sat on each side of a square, tiered fountain.

It was charming and very serene.

And without the presence of his nieces, very, very private.

Rourke let go of her elbow and faced her. "I want an heir."

She did a credible job of hiding her astonishment. "And you want the institute to assist with that? We specialize in IVF but we also have an excellent history with surrogacy." Or maybe he had a girlfriend that not even little Tanya knew about.

For some reason, her mouth tasted a little acid over that thought.

"I know."

Relief coursed through her. At least now she felt as if she understood what he was aiming for. He'd said he wanted an heir. A child. They could help to make that come about. "Confidentiality is sacred at the Armstrong Fertility Institute, Rourke. You don't have to worry about that. And honestly, my brother Paul might want to brain me for saying this, but you don't have to agree to invest this heavily just to be assured of that. In comparison, those fees would be—" She broke off, shrugging. Because, truly, those fees would be less than minuscule to a man of his significant wealth. "As for the surrogate, if you have someone in mind, our attorney will walk through the entire process with both of you. And if you don't have someone in mind, we have—"

"I do. You."

It took her a minute to realize what he'd said.

She pressed her hand to her chest, a disbelieving laugh on her lips. "You want *me* to be your surrogate?"

"No," he said evenly. "I want you to be my wife."

She felt the blood drain out of her head. Disbelief morphed into anger.

Clearly he wasn't serious. Nothing since she'd stepped into Fare for that farce of a meeting the day before had been serious.

Not to him.

Her hands curled at her sides. "I cannot believe I let myself take this seriously. When, obviously, this is all just a game to you. What is it, Rourke?" She spread her arms. "Do you have some particular ax to grind or are you just bored?"

He ignored her. "I figure a year, maybe two at the outside. That's comfortable enough to have a child within that time. After which you can go your way and I'll go mine. The child, of course, will be with me at least half the time. I'm not ignorant that two parents are better than one. If you choose to exercise that role, of course. If not—" He shrugged. "I'll be just as happy to have him or her full-time. As you've seen for yourself there's plenty of other family around."

She gaped. "You plan to push this theoretical child off on your mother to care for, just so you can have yourself an heir?"

"Of course not." He looked impatient. "My mother obviously adores her grandchildren, but I don't expect her to raise them. My mother lives here, but this is my home."

"But you have a penthouse in the city." The glorious penthouse that Sara Beth had raved over nearly as much as she'd raved over Ted, who'd romantically swept her there while he'd been courting her.

"And a lakeside loft in Chicago and a cabin in Colorado and a house on an Oregon cliff. All of which are beside the point. In exchange for your…contribution…the institute will receive all the funds it needs to climb back out of its hole and stay there."

"How generous." Her voice dripped sarcasm. "If you're serious—and frankly, I'm having a hard time with swallowing that—what on God's green earth would lead you to think that I'd be agreeable to this?"

"You told me yourself you're dedicated to the institute."

"Dedicated, yes. Insane, no."

"Then when you get back home, you'd better tell everyone at the institute to polish up their resumes."

"I'm sorry to bust your egotistical bubble, Mr. Devlin, but you are not the only player in the investment game. I'll find new investors. *Real* ones." Investors who weren't out of their minds. "Nobody at the institute is going to have to lose their jobs. Nobody!"

"If you don't agree, there's not an investor in this country—or beyond—who'll want to touch the Armstrong Fertility Institute when I'm finished." His voice was low. Flat. "Everyone—and I mean everyone—will know how badly your own brother embezzled from the company. Derek couldn't even stick to just draining from your operational funds. He had to take from the research grants, too. And he did it for *years,* right under your noses. You think you weathered tough times when the institute was accused of using unauthorized donor sperm and eggs? When you were accused of inflating the in vitro success ratios? That was a cakewalk. You don't have only patients to lose. You've got the respect of every medical and scientific community to lose. Everything your father ever worked for." His black gaze didn't waver. "The institute won't just disappear quietly into the night like a fine business that has seen a natural end of life. It'll blow up and the toxic fumes will never fade. Not even your very capable PR fixer, Ramona Tate, will be able to spin you out of this."

The chicken salad they'd had for lunch swirled nauseatingly inside her. "How did you know about Derek? From Ted?" She would have staked her reputation on Ted's loyalty to the institute.

She *had* staked her reputation on it.

The look Rourke gave her was almost pitying. "Ted Bonner has never betrayed anyone or anything, least of all the Armstrong Institute."

"Then how did you come across such privileged information?"

"There are some things that even the venerable Armstrong family can't hide," he said, leaning toward her. "Do you really think that I would consider investing in the institute without knowing exactly what I'd be getting into? I made it my business to know as soon as Ted called to set up a meeting with you. I didn't get to where I am by being naive, Lisa."

"Did you get there by resorting to blackmail to get what you want?" She was shaking and very much aware that he hadn't answered her. "Or are we just special that way?"

His smile was cold. The wolf in full, ravenous mode, greeting Red Riding Hood right at the door. "Oh, princess, you are definitely special. And don't consider it blackmail when we're all getting something we want out of the deal."

Fury bubbled inside her, vibrating through her voice. "You met me yesterday with no intention of investing."

He didn't deny it.

"So what happened between yesterday and today? Some angel visit you in your dreams and tell you it was time for an heir?" She struggled to keep her voice down.

His gaze drifted from her face, down her body, and back up again. "Something visited me in my dreams," he allowed.

There was no mistaking his implication and she flushed so hard, she was practically seeing him through crimson.

Or else that was her fury.

She'd never been so close to losing control. She wanted to yell and pound her hands on something.

He would make a satisfying target.

She took a deep breath, waiting until her vocal cords didn't feel as if they were strangling her. "I have no intention of being your broodmare, and even less intention of allowing you to ruin my institute!"

"You might want to think about it," he suggested, when she turned on her heel and started walking away from the fountain. "I'll give you until tomorrow afternoon. That'll give my media director time to leak the…appropriate news."

He'd been talking with his media director for much of their drive to Greenwich. She felt even sicker. She looked back at him. "Appropriate."

"Don't agree to my…proposal—"

"Proposal!" She snorted. "Insane proposition, maybe."

He barely paused over her interruption. "—and it'll be just as I've described. A hailstorm of disaster will come down on the institute by the time people tune into the evening news. But if you do agree, I'll work equally hard at ensuring the world never knows what sort of thievery you have going on in your family. And the only thing in the news will be a human interest blip about our upcoming marriage."

She hated, absolutely hated the fact that there was a stinging burn deep behind her eyes. There was no way she'd show any sort of weakness in front of this man. "Why should I trust you?"

He held up his hand. "Scout's honor."

She stared at him, her hands curling and uncurling at her sides. "I've never come as close to wanting to hit someone as I am now."

"Your brother Derek would make a better target." His voice was flat. "He's the one who put you in this position."

And how badly she wanted to be able to deny it.

But she couldn't.

Derek. Her own brother. The one she'd always been able to turn to. He'd been the one to teach her to drive when her father was too busy to and her mother was disinclined to. He'd been the one to help her pass her high-school math classes, to whisk her away for a day of sailing when all the rest of her friends were primping for the prom that she'd never been asked to go to. She'd gone to the same university as he; he'd told her what teachers were good and which ones to avoid. He'd taken her out for her first legal beer.

And he'd been her biggest supporter when it came to convincing their father that she—youngest of the Armstrong siblings—had what it took to become the head administrator of the institute.

She hated him for what he'd done to all of them. Couldn't understand how he could have done what he'd done.

And she wished like hell that she could cut off the memory of all that he'd meant to her.

"Come on, Lisa." Rourke's voice dropped gently; the

predator sensing weakness. "It won't be so bad. A handful of years at the outside is all you'll be giving up. And in exchange, the institute will be set for the next fifty years when the next generation takes over. You can expand. Open another location on the west coast if you want. The sky will be the limit."

She didn't care about expansion. Or new sites. She cared about the site—the only site—they had. She cared about what it would do to her father if the institute fell from grace while it was under her watch. Gerald's health had been declining for years. She wasn't sure if he could survive such a mammoth, shocking disappointment.

She and Paul and the others at the institute had all agreed that it was best to keep Derek's horrible misdeeds from their parents. It wouldn't solve anything if they knew, and would only upset them.

She pressed her fingers to her temples.

But if Rourke was to be believed—if she didn't go along with his plan—there was no way that her parents wouldn't learn what Derek had done.

It was unbearable to even contemplate.

"My driver can take you back to your hotel," Rourke said, and she decided she was losing her mind to think there was a hint of compassion in his voice. "You have some thinking to do."

"According to you, there's no thinking to be done. Agree or suffer the consequences."

"The institute can't hide its financial precariousness much longer. Even if I did nothing, the truth would come out."

"But you're prepared to help it along." Her voice was thick. She looked at him, wishing she could understand what was ticking behind his impenetrable gaze. "And for what? What did we ever do to you?"

His eyes narrowed. "I don't like thieves."

"I don't like drivers who run red lights," she exclaimed.

"But I don't take it so personally that I deliberately go hunting them down!"

"I didn't hunt you down, sweetheart. *You* came to me. I've just come up with a solution that benefits us both."

She shook her head. His gall was unbelievable. "You can whitewash it all you want, Rourke, but coercion is still coercion."

He sighed faintly. "The more you keep thinking along those lines, the harder this all will be. My advice to you is to focus on the advantages." His lips twisted a little. "That's what I'm doing."

She watched him.

The silence between them slowly ticked along, broken only by the soft gurgle of water spilling tranquilly over the edges of the fountain.

"I don't see why we would have to marry," she finally said. Maybe…*maybe*…she could tolerate being a surrogate mother for him. But that didn't necessitate a pointless marriage.

A glint sparked in his eyes. The wolf scenting blood. "My child won't be born a bastard."

She looked up at the blue sky, then back at him. "Come out of the Dark Ages," she said impatiently. "People hardly care about that anymore!"

"My mother still cares." His expression was inflexible. "I care."

So they'd all suffer through a sham of a marriage just so his heir wouldn't be born out of wedlock?

"I suppose I should be grateful you don't have some moral objection to divorce, too!"

"If I did, it went by the wayside well enough thanks to my ex-wife."

She'd been aware that he was divorced, yet her furtive research when she'd first met him hadn't managed to unearth any details about the woman. He'd been paired with dozens of women—from famous models to actresses to heiresses. But there'd definitely been no details of his former wife. "How long ago were you married?" Maybe he was nursing a broken heart and taking it out on her because she was female.

"A lifetime."

"Right." He wasn't that old. Only four years older than she. "What happened?"

"Nothing that concerns you."

"It does if I'm going to be putting your ring on my finger," she returned. "Since I assume, to go along with your other antiquated notions, that you'll be wanting me to wear one."

"You think it's old-fashioned for a couple to exchange rings along with their vows?"

She wanted to stomp her foot. Because she *didn't* think it was old-fashioned. She thought it was right and it was true and it was what people *in love* did. People who were committing themselves to each other for the rest of their lives.

Like Sara Beth and Ted had done. Like Paul and Ramona were going to be doing.

Certainly not for Rourke and her.

The very idea of it struck her as blasphemous.

"There is just one more detail," he added.

Her nerves tightened until they vibrated at a screaming pitch. "What?"

"The terms of our arrangement are to be kept private. As far as the rest of the world will know—including your family and your friends as well as mine—this will be a traditional marriage. Entered into for all of the traditional reasons."

She let out a disbelieving laugh. "Like what? Love? Who's going to believe that we're in love?"

His gaze suddenly focused on her mouth. His voice dropped. "I think we can be convincing enough."

She felt scorched and wanted badly to blame it on her temper. On the impossible position he was forcing her into.

But she was fresh out of strength to even maintain that simple of a lie to herself.

"What if I have a problem carrying the baby?" She tossed out the possibility with a hint of desperation. The fertilization itself wouldn't be a problem. Obviously. In vitro fertilization—IVF—was just one of the specialties at the institute.

But carrying the baby to term once it was implanted?

Her sister, Olivia, was proof that not every pregnancy made it to term. Who was she to say that she might not have Olivia's tendency toward miscarriage?

But even as she thought it, her common sense rejected it. Physically, Olivia was as delicate as an orchid. Her sister's body simply wasn't built to bear children. Lisa was about as delicate as an oak tree.

"You're in excellent health," he said. "There's no reason to believe you would have difficulty."

"How do you know I'm in excellent health?" Her jaw tightened. "Maybe I...maybe I have an STD!"

He laughed softly. "How long has it been since you've been with a man?"

She flushed. There was no earthly way that Rourke could know that she hadn't been involved with anyone—that way—since she'd been in college. Years. Followed by more years. "None of your business."

"It is when you're going to be carrying my baby inside of you."

Her knees felt weak. She moved around him—uncaring that he seemed to find amusement in the distance she kept between them—and sat down on one of the carved benches.

"It's academic, anyway," he commented. He plucked a leaf from the hedge nearest him and twirled it between his fingers.

A distant part of her brain envied him that ability to look so calm when everything was going to hell in a handbasket.

"It doesn't matter how many lovers you've had," he went on. "Or haven't had. You had your annual physical last month just like you've done for years. You're as healthy as a horse. You don't even have a prescription for birth control pills."

Her jaw dropped. "How do you know that?"

He just continued watching her. Leaving her with mad scenarios of stolen medical files running rampant through her head. But that would have taken forethought, wouldn't it?

She eyed him, not certain of anything anymore. "You've thought of everything, I guess."

"And now it's time for you to do your thinking."

But she just shook her head and looked away from him. "There is no choice." And he knew it.

"You'll do what it takes to save the institute?"

He let go of the leaf. Her eyes watched it swirl around in circles until it landed on the gravel between them.

"Yes." She looked up at him. "You've got a deal."

Chapter Four

Rourke watched the limousine bearing Lisa in the rear seat drive away from the house.

A part of him was elated.

An equal part of him was disgusted.

Not with Lisa. She'd done exactly what he'd expected her to do. His personal dealings with her might have been counted on one hand, but he knew she was singularly dedicated in her goals where the institute was concerned. Agreeing to his terms had been her only option.

He wished that the elation could edge out the disgust if only for a moment or two.

"Where'd Lisa go?"

He looked over at Tricia, who'd walked around to the front of the house. "She has to catch a flight back to Boston."

After she'd agreed, she'd asked him about the rest of his plans.

And even though he had more than a few, he hadn't been able to heap them on top of her slightly bowed shoulders. So he'd lied. He'd told her that he would contact her later and they could iron out the details.

Her lips had twisted. But when she'd pushed off the bench, she'd stood tall and slender in front of him when she'd told him that she would use his limo then, after all.

Because she had work to get back to.

He knew there was no doubting that.

Even with him throwing money at the institute, it was going to take some real work to recover from the mess that Derek Armstrong had left behind.

He shoved his hands in his pockets, willfully pushing all thoughts of the man out of his head. He looked at Tricia. "What did you think of her?"

His sister—only two years his junior—looked up at him. "What do you think I thought? She looks like Taylor."

He turned to look back at the curving drive, though the limousine had already passed from sight. That had been his first thought, too, when he'd seen Lisa in Shots. That she looked like his faithless ex-wife. But the next time he'd seen her—when Ted and Sara Beth had eloped—he'd realized how superficial that first, startling resemblance had been. Oh, Lisa was still slender and leggy. A blonde with brown eyes and a face that was arrestingly sculptured with a reserved demeanor that just begged to be smashed.

"She's not Taylor," he told his sister. She might be an ice princess, but Lisa had a brain. And dedication, which she'd proved just that afternoon.

The only dedication his ex had was to herself.

"Well, obviously, I know that," Tricia said, rolling her eyes. "Just make sure you remember it."

"What else did you think of her?"

She eyed him more closely. With all the suspicion of a sister who'd endured plenty from him throughout their childhood. "She seems nice enough. A little cool, but I think that's probably because she's shy."

"Shy?" He shook his head, dismissing the notion. Lisa had confidence to spare. There was no room for shyness there. "Not a chance."

His sister huffed. "Why'd you ask if you're going to ignore what I think, anyway? Trust me. The woman has a shy streak a half mile wide. You just don't see it 'cause you're a guy. All *you* see are those long legs of hers and those big brown eyes."

He saw a lot more than that. He saw the means to his future. One that, for a long while, he'd given up on ever having.

He never thought he'd be in the position of hearing his own biological clock ticking, but that was where he was. There was a helluva lot of macabre irony that the situation caused by Derek Armstrong was now providing Rourke with the means to succeed in the one thing he'd ever failed at.

Or maybe, it was simply poetic justice.

Elation edged ahead at last, and Rourke dropped his arm over his sister's shoulder. "How fast do you think you can put together a wedding?"

Lisa stood on the front porch of her parents' home and took a deep breath. She'd barely landed in Boston when her cell phone started ringing with messages, but it was the one from her mother that had brought Lisa here this evening.

Nobody ignored Emily when she summoned you to a family dinner.

Not even when one had, just that day, been coerced into agreeing to marry a devil.

Blowing out a breath, she pushed open the door, entering the foyer where the scent of furniture polish and fresh flowers greeted her. Knowing that her mother wouldn't appreciate her arriving with briefcase in hand—tangible evidence that she was a businesswoman and not a society wife—she left it on the floor next to an antique console table that held the cut-crystal vase filled with flowers and walked through the house that she'd grown up in.

She found everyone already in the drawing room. Her mother was sitting on the settee, her typical glass of sherry in her hand. Surprisingly, Gerald was out of bed and sat in his wheelchair next to the settee, sipping amber liquid from a squat glass of his own. Paul and his fiancée, Ramona, were standing close together near the bay window that overlooked the back of the estate. Her blond head was tilted close to his dark one and they seemed lost in their own world.

Derek was notably absent, for which Lisa was painfully grateful.

She was pretty certain that in her present mood, she would have lost her control altogether if she'd had to see him just then.

It was going to be difficult enough trying to sell the idea of her sudden "romance" with Rourke Devlin as it was.

She went to her father first, bending over him to kiss his cheek. "Daddy. It's good to see you up. You're looking well." And he did. His shoulders weren't as broad and strong as they'd been before he'd become confined to his wheelchair and his face wasn't as fiercely handsome as it had once been, but he was still an impressive, dauntingly intelligent man.

And right now, that intelligence was peering out at her from her father's eyes. "You don't," he said bluntly. "What's wrong?"

"Nothing!" She straightened and managed a laugh. "Just too much to do and not enough hours in the day. That's what *you* always used to say," she reminded.

He lifted his glass, watching her over the rim. He didn't look convinced, but she turned quickly for her customary air-kiss with her mother.

"You're late," was the only observation her mother had for her.

"I'm sorry." She looked over the back of the settee to find her brother watching her, his eyebrows lifted a little.

She could well imagine he was curious about the results of her New York trip. She shook her head ever so slightly, glancing back at her mother. "You know I was in New York for most of the day. I had to stop at the institute when I got back."

Emily's lips pursed. "I suppose that's why you didn't have time to dress more appropriately for dinner."

She was long used to her mother's disapproval and ignored it in favor of going to the gleaming wooden bar on the far side of the room. "I thought Olivia and her clan would be here, too," she said to no one in particular.

"She and Jamison had another function tonight."

And of course those functions would be important enough not to earn Emily's trademarked sniff of displeasure. "Too bad," Lisa said. "I was looking forward to seeing Kevin and Danny again." Since they'd joined the family, Lisa had been unfailingly charmed by the two sweet little boys her sister and brother-in-law had adopted. And right now, the three- and seven-year-olds would have provided a welcome distraction. "How long until dinner?"

She could hear her mother's sigh from across the room. "Long enough for you to have an aperitif."

As if to *not* have a pre-dinner drink was the height of crassness.

Paul appeared beside her and pulled a wineglass from beneath the bar. "White?"

She stifled her own sigh and nodded.

He poured her a glass. "I'm sorry I was tied up with patients this afternoon and missed you when you got back." His voice was low. "How'd it go?"

Her fingers tightened nervously around the delicate crystal stemware. Her mother had switched her attention to fussing over Gerald, though Ramona was watching them. Lisa pulled her lips into a smile for her brother and his fiancée, lifting her glass a little as if in a toast. "We…um…we're not going to have to worry about that…small problem anymore. It's completely taken care of." Or it would be soon enough.

She took a hasty gulp, drowning her anxiety in wine.

"He went for it, then?"

He, of course, meant Rourke. "Mmm-hmm."

Her brother smiled. "I knew you could pull it off, Lis."

"There is one thing I need to tell you—" She broke off when they heard the chimes ringing from the front doorbell. Her first thought was that Derek was showing up, after all, but she quickly dismissed it. This was his childhood home, too. He wouldn't have stood on ceremony any more than she had. He'd have walked right on in.

"Go see who it is, Lisa," her mother ordered. "Anna is off today." Anna was her parents' housekeeper.

She didn't mind. It gave her an escape for at least a few minutes. She left her wineglass sitting on the bar and walked through the house back to the front door, pulling it open without so much as a glance through the heavily leaded sidelights.

Rourke stood on the porch. He was wearing a dark overcoat that made his shoulders look even wider than usual, and the golden light from the sconces positioned beside the massive door made his black hair glint.

She resolutely ignored the way her heart practically stood still and pulled the door shut a little behind her, lest anyone else's curiosity led them to the foyer. "What are *you* doing here?"

"Is that any way to greet your fiancé?"

The term jarred her. "What would you like me to do? Throw myself into your arms?"

"That'd be more natural, wouldn't it?"

"There's nothing *natural* about any of this." The magnitude of what she'd agreed to overwhelmed her all over again. As did the needlessness of it all. She stepped farther outside, nearly pulling the door closed entirely. "Why me?" she asked. "If you want a child—within the bounds of wedlock," she added quickly before he could interrupt, "why not just marry one of your other women?"

He smiled a little. "And what women would those be?"

The evening air was decidedly cool, but her limbs felt decidedly not. "The women you date. Obviously." He was a seriously eligible bachelor. There was no question that the man had women in his life.

"Dating gets…messy."

Wasn't that what she believed, herself?

"This feels pretty messy to me," she countered.

"This is business. The terms are already outlined."

"A child is not a business."

"So says the woman whose entire life revolves around an institute that creates them."

"We're not cloning people, for heaven's sake! We're helping infertile couples achieve fertility." She went stock-still when his hand suddenly lifted toward her.

"This strand of hair keeps working loose of that knot you keep it in." His knuckles brushed the underside of her jaw as he ran his thumb and forefinger down the long, wavy lock.

It didn't seem to matter that he was wreaking havoc on her life. Just that faint touch made her bones feel like gel. "Wh-what are you doing here? For that matter, how'd you even know where I was?"

He wound the strands of hair around his finger. "Your assistant told me."

She jerked back, and he let her hair loose though he still left her feeling crowded on what was supposed to be a very spacious porticoed entrance. "What were you doing calling Ella?"

"Finding out your schedule, obviously."

"You should have contacted me."

He smiled faintly. "Somehow, I think Ella was more forthcoming than you would have been."

The truth of that stuck in her throat. "You said we…we would work out the details of our—" She couldn't even manage an appropriate word and just waved her hand instead. "Later."

"And now it's later. You're meeting with your family this evening. I figured it'd be logical for me to be here when you tell them we're getting married."

"Maybe I didn't plan to tell them this evening," she bluffed. Badly.

"I'd think you'd rather they hear it from you than from somewhere else."

"What'd you do? Issue a press release?" She hadn't really taken him seriously on that score.

"I've arranged for the ceremony to be held in New York at St. Patrick's Cathedral."

"What?" The cathedral was famous. It was Catholic. "I'm not Catholic." She hadn't even been to church in years. And he was a divorced man.

"I am."

She folded her arms tightly. "Aren't there…requirements to be met there? Marriage classes or something?"

"Ordinarily."

How simply he glossed over what she knew had to be an encyclopedia of protocols, and it was just another example that he wasn't any ordinary man. Not even an ordinary, wealthy man.

So she squashed the multitude of questions that her detail-oriented mind wanted answers for, and settled for just one. "Why do you want a church ceremony when you've already promised that our…union…has an expiration date?"

"That's a promise known only between you and me, remember? As far as anyone else is concerned, this is the real deal. Unless you're already chickening out."

She made a face. "I'm not chickening out." Not because she didn't want to back out. She did. But she wanted to ensure the institute's security even more.

"Good." He slid his hand inside the pocket of his coat and he pulled out a small, square jeweler's box. Without ceremony, he thumbed it open and pulled out a diamond ring. "Put this on."

She eyed the simple, emerald-cut solitaire. If this were a real engagement—if she were head over heels in love with the man—she would have been bowled over by its exquisite beauty. Something she would have chosen for herself—albeit a more modest-size stone—if she were given the opportunity.

But in that sense, there was nothing real about any of this.

She took the ring and slid it onto her left ring finger. The narrow band fit a little loosely and she nudged it with her thumb, pushing the weighty diamond to the center.

Beautiful or not, the ring felt more like a noose around her neck.

"I suppose you've already decided what date, too?"

"Next week."

She nearly reeled. "So soon?"

"I can fit it into my schedule now. And yours, as it happens, since you'll be able to cancel all of those meetings you have lined up next week with potential investors."

"H-how did you arrange the cathedral on such short notice?"

"I asked."

Panic bloomed inside her head. How could she ever be a match against him?

"Everything is already arranged," he continued. "The ceremony will be at four. We'll have a small reception afterward at my penthouse. It's easier than finding another suitable venue, and Raoul will provide the catering. All you have to do is find a gown. We'll issue a few official photographs for the press, so keep that in mind."

"I'm surprised you didn't take care of the gown, then, too."

"Your taste is excellent. But if you prefer, I can make a few calls to some designers I know."

"Gosh. Thanks." She shivered and her sarcasm was shaky.

"You're cold." He suddenly pulled her close to him, wrapping his overcoat around her.

It was like being engulfed by a blast furnace. And for the life of her, she couldn't pull away.

"Better?" His voice dropped, whispering against her temple.

Her fingers curled against his shoulders, easily discerning the hard feel of him beneath the soft wool. No extra padding in that coat, at all. "Not really," she admitted.

"It won't all be bad. Have you seen the Mediterranean?"

She shook her head. She had to fight against the urge to lean against him. To just let him take her weight, and everything else on her plate....

But wasn't that what he was doing, anyway?

"I've arranged a private villa in the French Riviera for the honeymoon."

Honeymoon. She almost laughed. Or cried. Because he was covering all of his bases as far as appearances went. "I don't want to be away from the office for even a week."

"You will be, and it'll be three weeks."

Her gaze flew to his. "That's impossible. I can't just flit off for—" She broke off when the door behind them opened again.

"What on earth is taking so…" Emily's voice trailed off at the sight that met her. "Long?" Her eyebrows lifted in silent demand.

Lisa tried to untangle herself from Rourke's arms, but he wasn't cooperating. Which left her to peer over his shoulder at her mother. But when she opened her mouth to explain, nothing came. "I…I—"

"Blame it on me, Mrs. Armstrong," Rourke said smoothly. Without releasing Lisa, he tucked her against his side and turned to face Emily, his hand extended. "It's good to meet you again."

Again? Startled, Lisa looked from his face to her mother's.

The insistent inquiry on Emily's face was replaced by surprise. And no small amount of confusion. "Mr. Devlin. How nice to see you."

"Your mother and I were on the same charitable board a few years ago," he told Lisa. The smile he directed at Emily was both rueful and charming. "I'm afraid I forgot to mention it before." He looked at Lisa, the very picture of devoted man. "We've been busy with…other matters."

Her cheeks burned. She wondered if he'd studied the way Ted Bonner was always looking at Sara Beth, because he had the whole besotted thing down to an art. She glanced at her mother, who was now eyeing her with even more surprise.

"*You* are…seeing…Rourke Devlin?"

She would have had to have been a stone to miss her mother's implication.

Her chin lifted. She smiled a little and let her left hand slide down to the center of Rourke's chest. There was no way that her mother could miss the diamond on her finger. "Yes."

Emily's lips parted. She blinked a little. And Lisa knew that she probably should be ashamed of enjoying, just a little, the sight of her mother so obviously at a loss for words.

"I hope you don't mind that I didn't speak to you and Dr. Armstrong before now," Rourke smoothly stepped into the verbal void. "But your daughter has a way of making me forget all convention."

Lisa nearly choked over that.

But Emily was recovering quickly. Her smile was still more than a little puzzled. Proof that she couldn't understand what appeal Lisa might have for a man like him. But she stepped back in the doorway, extending her hand. "Of course we don't mind," she was saying. "Lisa is an adult. She makes her own decisions. Now come in out of the chill. We've got most of the family here," she continued when Rourke let go of Lisa and nudged her back inside the house. "Though it would have been perfect if Derek and Olivia could have been here for such an announcement." She gave Lisa a censorious look, as if Lisa had deliberately chosen the timing to annoy her.

But there was nothing but delighted pleasure again in Emily's face when she pushed the door closed and tucked her arm through Rourke's to lead him through her graciously decorated home.

Following behind them, Lisa blew out a silent breath.

At least now she didn't have to figure out a way to break the unlikely news that she was going to marry the man.

In that, she supposed she ought to be grateful.

"Everyone, look who's here." Emily's voice had taken on a cheerful slant by the time they entered the drawing room. "Darling." She went first to Gerald. "You remember Rourke Devlin, don't you?"

Rourke shook the older man's hand. "It's good to see you, Dr. Armstrong."

Gerald waved that off. "Gerald," he insisted. "And of course I remember the last time." He sounded irritated that Emily might suggest he wouldn't. "He was at the Founder's

Ball. Lisa, get the man a drink." He gestured to the leather chair that until a few years ago, had been his own preferred perch. "You've met my eldest son, Paul, and his fiancée?"

Aware of the surprised looks that were passing between her brother and Ramona as the two greeted Rourke, Lisa went to the bar. She couldn't very well ask Rourke what he preferred to drink—presumably that would be something a "normal" fiancée would know—so she poured him a glass of the same wine she was drinking.

Though, as she carried it over to him and he tugged her down onto the arm of the chair and held her there with his implacable hand around her hips, she was rather wishing that she'd chosen a much stronger drink for herself. Instead, she held her own glass with tight fingers and it was then—seemingly all at once—that the rest of them noticed the ring on her finger.

Ramona gasped.

Paul muttered an uncharacteristic oath.

And Gerald just slapped his hand on his thigh. "Well, my God, Lisa-girl. Aren't you full of surprises!"

She smiled, hoping it didn't look as weak as it felt, and avoided her brother's eyes. Of all those present, he was the one least likely to be convinced about her and Rourke's sudden match. "Wait until you hear Rourke's plans for the wedding," she said and smiled down at her intended bride-groom with a sudden hint of sadistic relish.

Let *him* be the one to tell Emily Stanton Armstrong that the wedding was already in the works.

And she'd have no say in the details, whatsoever.

"My pleasure," he said smoothly. But instead of launching into the litany of wedding arrangements that he'd already, arrogantly made, he lifted her free hand and pressed his thumb unerringly against her erratic pulse.

Then he smiled a little and sent her brief little spurt of

satisfaction packing when he pressed his mouth slowly, intentionally, against her palm.

She forgot about her mother and everyone else. Except Rourke. And the fact that he'd plucked all control right out of the hand he was kissing.

Chapter Five

"You look beautiful." Lisa's sister, Olivia, fussed for a moment with the lightweight veil that streamed down Lisa's back from the small jeweled clasp where it fastened around her low chignon. "This has got to be one of the most romantic marriages I've ever heard of." Her dark eyes met Lisa's as she squeezed her hand. "This has been a remarkable year. I'm so happy for you and Rourke."

"Thanks." Lisa stared at herself in the long mirror of the luxurious hotel suite where she'd spent the night before her wedding. She'd traveled from Boston just yesterday morning and, in the thirty-six hours since, had been pinned and tucked into the wedding gown that she now wore, and her body from head to toe had been primped and fussed over by a crew of hairdressers, masseuses and aestheticians. And not two hours earlier, all buffed and polished, she'd stood in her perfectly fitted ivory gown on the terrace of her beautiful suite for the formal portrait that her mother had insisted upon. She'd been catered to and fussed over, and if she'd been given her fondest wish, she would have been miles and miles away from all of it.

There was something really wrong with surrounding herself with all the trappings of a fairy-tale wedding when the reason for it in the first place was anything but a fairy-tale romance. Lisa kept waiting for someone to stop and point them out as the counterfeit couple that they were, only nobody did.

Not Rourke's family, who'd hosted the rehearsal dinner the evening before at an unexpectedly quaint, homey Italian restaurant that Lisa had learned had once belonged to his grandparents, but was now run by Lea, mother of the impish Tanya. And definitely not by Lisa's parents. Emily might have been frustrated by her inability to run what she considered "her" territory—her daughter's wedding—but she was nevertheless glorying in the fact that Lisa was making such an unexpectedly advantageous match.

Lisa dragged her thoughts together. "And, you know, thanks for being my matron of honor," she offered to her sister. Olivia looked ethereal in her close-fitting royal-blue gown. Thanks to being Mrs. Jamison Mallory, she hadn't needed to prevail upon any of Rourke's connections to come up with an outfit befitting the occasion. "I know it was short notice."

Olivia laughed a little. "I'm glad to do it, Lisa." She swept a slender hand down her tea-length skirt. "Actually, I assumed you'd want Sara Beth to stand up with you. You're so close."

Lisa would have been glad for her best friend's support even if Sara Beth didn't know the full details of her and Rourke's arrangement. But Sara Beth had already been with Lisa for much of the day. She'd arrived at the hotel that morning before the buffers and the polishers with a bottle of champagne and a determination to see Lisa through what she suspected wasn't the "perfect romance" that had been touted in the news as soon as the media got a whiff of Rourke Devlin's impending nuptials.

But now, Sara Beth was already at the cathedral, giving support to her husband who was serving as Rourke's best man.

"I love Sara Beth, too. But you're my sister," Lisa said.

Olivia looked touched. "Well. Don't make my mascara run now, when it's time for us to leave for the ceremony. I hope that Jamison hasn't let Kevin lose the rings." She turned to retrieve the orchid bouquets that had been delivered to Lisa's suite earlier. "He's so excited about being the ring bearer but I think a lot of it may have to do with getting to walk beside Chance's stepdaughter, Annie. He's fascinated with her red hair."

Panic rippled through Lisa's stomach, and it had nothing to do with either Kevin or little Annie. With Olivia's attention elsewhere, she quickly swallowed down the last of her champagne. Courage, even in liquid form, seemed definitely called for.

Then she hefted up her trailing gown and took her bouquet from her sister. Like it or not, it was showtime.

Rourke pulled back his cuff and looked at his watch.

"Don't worry." Ted clapped him on the back. "The Plaza is only minutes away. She'll be here."

"I know. I just want to get it over with."

Ted smiled. "And get on with the wedding night?"

Rourke didn't deny it. He hadn't told his old friend any of the details behind the sudden marriage; leaving intact Ted's assumption that Rourke's interest in Lisa had carried them away.

The pretense wasn't entirely a pretense, anyway. Since that night with Lisa at her parents' home, he hadn't seen her again until the previous day when they'd both put their signatures on his prenup before joining the rest of their families and friends for the rehearsal and the dinner following.

Holding her in his arms, dropping kisses on her lips. None of it had been a hardship and if anything, he *was* more than a little preoccupied with thoughts of what was to come after the "I do's" were said.

"Gentlemen?" The woman in charge of keeping them on time poked her head into the room where Ted and Rourke were waiting. "We're ready for you."

Ted grinned and gave him a thumbs-up before preceding him to the chapel. The organist was already playing when he and Ted lined up in front of the priest.

He was surprised to feel a jolt of nervousness when he turned to wait for his bride. It wasn't a common sensation. His mother sat in the front pew, beaming her pleasure at him. Behind her were his sisters and their husbands and broods. Tanya was bouncing in her seat, alternating between pouts and smiles. She'd given him hell the evening before for stooping to marry someone else before she became available.

Young Kevin Jamison appeared, his focus much more squarely on the pillow he was carrying which bore the wedding rings, than it was on where he was walking. Fortunately, his sidekick, Annie Labeaux—who was practically preening in her ruffled yellow dress—knew her marks perfectly, and kept Kevin coming in a forward motion.

Then Lisa's sister appeared, gliding up the aisle like the dancer he knew she'd once been. Tanya bounced again and, despite her mother's grasping hands, managed to stand up on her pew to wave both hands at him.

He waved back, earning a soft chuckle from most of the guests. But he wasn't really listening because Lisa had appeared at the rear of the chapel.

Rourke was vaguely aware of Gerald accompanying her

in his wheelchair along the aisle toward him. Vaguely aware of the change in the organ music. Vaguely aware that he was still breathing.

She was beautiful.

Draped in some airy fabric that cinched her narrow waist in bits of lace, managing to look painfully innocent and wrenchingly sexy at the same time.

Her eyes didn't meet his when she reached the end of the aisle. She kissed her father's cheek and his motorized chair silently left her side.

Leaving Lisa to *him*.

He could see her pulse beating at the base of her slender neck. See a similar beat in the smooth flesh between the modest *V* of her neckline. And he could feel it beneath his fingers in her hands after she handed off her bouquet to her sister and placed them, cool and slightly shaking, in his.

Later, he knew they'd both repeated the vows. Knew he'd pushed his platinum band on her finger and had donned the wider version of it for himself. He knew that she'd lifted her lips for his brief kiss when the priest called for it, and knew that she'd tucked her hand through his arm as they'd walked back down the chapel aisle.

He knew it, because the license was duly signed afterward, they blinked against the flash of a dozen cameras as they left the cathedral behind, and then they were inside his limousine, which was bearing them, right on schedule, back to his Park Avenue apartment. The rest of the wedding party and guests were following in a raft of identical stretches.

"So that's it," she said, as they left the cathedral behind. She was looking at her hands that were splayed flat on her lap, surrounded by the cloud of her long gown.

Probably looking at the wedding rings.

"That was just the start."

He watched her fingers curl into the airy gown until neither her fingers nor the rings were visible. She looked straight ahead at the smoked privacy window separating them from the driver, then turned her head to look out the window. Her veil was pulled to one side, exposing her pale nape and the small, lone freckle that graced the tender skin.

He would kiss that freckle soon enough. And every inch of creamy flesh that stretched down her spine. He wondered how long it would take to undo the dozens of tiny diamond-like buttons that stretched down the back of her gown. Wondered, too, what she would be wearing beneath it.

She looked at him suddenly, her eyes narrowed, as if she'd been reading his mind. But she quickly disabused him of that notion. "There's not going to be any photographers at your apartment, are there?"

"At the reception?" He shook his head. "No. Outside the building, though? Likely." There had been a few camped out there for the past several days, clearly documenting the somewhat surprising fact that Rourke Devlin's fiancée wasn't yet in residence. "Don't worry. You're the picture of a princess bride. Just look up at me adoringly as we go inside and every-one'll be happy."

She grimaced and looked back out the window again. "Everyone but us," she muttered. "Even my best friend doesn't know what a lie this all is. I hope you're planning on going to confession someday or that farce of a wedding ceremony will haunt us to hell."

He touched his finger to her arm, feeling her start, before he dragged it slowly down to her wrist. "That's how you saw it?"

She shifted, crossing her arms. "How could I not? It was a pretense. Love, honor and cherish?" She shook her head, the corner of her lips turned downward.

"You'll be my wife with all the respect that deserves. I'll

honor you." And he'd cherish her body the second he had the chance. No question.

The line of her jaw was like a finely chiseled masterpiece. "You won't love me."

Love had never gotten him anywhere. "And you won't love me."

She slid him an icy look. "That's right. The sooner we get what we want out of this deal, the happier I'll be."

"Then we're in agreement." He held her gaze with his, even after the limo sighed to a stop in front of his building. "Now, are you ready to get on with this?" His driver opened the door next to him.

Lisa's gaze slipped away. She picked up her bouquet that had been lying on the seat between them and nodded.

He stepped out of the car, and turned to help her out. She stuck out one slender foot, shod in delicate straps, and then the dress seemed to follow as she slid out of the vehicle.

It was like watching flower petals unfurl and he knew the photographers that—as predicted—were still camped out nearby would be snapping away.

The moment Lisa was standing beside him, he slid his arm around her waist and pulled her close. His mouth covered hers.

Her lips parted; he could taste her quick word of protest, but he ignored it. And then he could taste the faint hint of champagne on her tongue and then deeper, the taste of *her* as she was kissing him back.

"Time enough for that later." Ted's laughing voice barely penetrated the fog that was gathering in Rourke's head. The hand his friend clamped on his shoulder was more intrusive.

Rourke slowly pulled away.

Lisa's eyes were wide. Her cheeks were flushed.

Sara Beth danced around next to Lisa, sliding a short little capelike thing around her shoulders that matched Lisa's dress before scurrying her toward the building, chattering a mile a minute about God only knew what. Crushed orchids rained down from Lisa's bouquet onto the sidewalk as they went.

He forced a smile for Ted and the others who were rapidly disgorging from the stream of limousines but the only thing he really saw was the panicked glance Lisa tossed back at him the moment before she disappeared into the building.

Yeah, he'd given the photographers their money shot, but just then he wasn't certain who was paying the price.

Lisa leaned back against the elevator wall and stared at her hands. She hadn't even had time to get used to the weight of the engagement ring during the past week, and now there was another band there to add to the unsettling unfamiliarity.

"Some kiss."

She glanced up at Sara Beth, who was not doing even a credible job of sounding, or looking, casual.

Lisa pressed her lips together for a moment. She could still taste him. "Yes." She kept her voice low. The elevator doors were still open. There was no point in pushing the button for Rourke's floor, because that particular one required a key.

Sara Beth's voice was just as low. "Considering the steam radiating off the two of you, I would've expected you to look a little more...glowing." She plucked Lisa's somewhat smashed bouquet out of her hands and gently stroked her hand over the blooms. "Rourke's obviously crazy about you. But are you really okay with this marriage thing? It's awfully sudden."

"I told you back at the hotel that I was."

"Yes, and you were two glasses into a bottle of champagne before you managed to say that." Sara Beth lifted her chin and smiled a little stiffly when Emily and Ramona stepped onto the elevator followed soon by Gerald, whose chair was being pushed by Paul.

"I still don't know why Derek wasn't at the ceremony," Emily was complaining. "I've left him a half-dozen messages but he hasn't called me back."

"Maybe he had something else he couldn't get out of," Paul said, his voice even.

"Not even for his sister's wedding?" Emily shook her head, looking upset.

"It was short notice for everyone, Mother," Lisa reminded, hoping that would be the end of it.

She had made it a point *not* to invite Derek and, considering the number of phone messages he'd been leaving for her, had been half afraid he'd show up anyway. Unless he was living under a rock, he couldn't fail to have read or heard that she was marrying the handsome billionaire.

Then Ted arrived, holding up a key that he used to unlock the button for the penthouse floor. "Rourke's talking to security. They were supposed to have the elevators unlocked by the time we got here."

"No detail left unturned," Lisa muttered.

Her mother leaned over to pinch Lisa's cheeks and she jerked back. "Hey."

"You need some color in your cheeks," Emily defended. "You're almost as white as your dress."

"I think she looks perfect," Ramona inserted, giving Lisa a quick wink when Emily turned to fuss over Gerald.

The elevator let them off in a spacious, marble-floored hallway that possessed two grand doors at opposite ends. The door belonging to Rourke was obvious; it was opened and a sedately uniformed beauty stood beside it, bearing a silver tray of crystal champagne flutes.

It took only a moment for Lisa to recognize the girl as the hostess from Raoul's restaurant. "For the new Mrs. Devlin," she greeted her, holding out her tray.

Mrs. Devlin.

Lisa's hand shook as she took one of the exquisitely cut stems. "Thank you."

"For heaven's sake, Lisa, we're not going to stand out here." Emily glided past, taking a glass of champagne for herself and Gerald, and entered the apartment with none of the reluctance that Lisa was trying to hide.

The second elevator arrived with a soft chime and, half afraid it would be bearing Rourke, she gathered her dress and went inside.

Even though she had been prepped by Sara Beth, who had seen the place when Ted had brought her here for a romantic getaway, Lisa still wasn't prepared for her first sight of Rourke's city home.

In its way it was as grand as his Greenwich estate. But where that mansion looked to have been steeped in tradition, his penthouse dripped modernism from its bank of unadorned windows to the gleaming dark wood floor, and minimalist ivory-colored furnishings.

The only color of note came exclusively from the chest-high glass vases flanking every window that were filled with immense bouquets of purple irises that seemed to reach for the high, coffered ceiling. The flowers were repeated in squat glass bowls all around the spacious living area.

She didn't know what surprised her more. The sleek, urban decor, or the profusion of flowers that he'd clearly arranged just for the purpose of their so-called reception.

"I told you it was beautiful," Sara Beth whispered beside her. She tucked her arm through Lisa's and drew her through the living area that was long enough to encompass Lisa's entire town house, toward the terrace beyond the windows where the flowers were even more resplendent.

Stunned, Lisa slowly stepped outside. There were several

tables set there arranged end to end and looking as if they'd come straight out of a photo shoot from a high-end wedding. Situated in the corner, there was even a harpist whose dulcet sounds trickled in the air. "Amazing," she murmured.

"Thanks." Rourke's sister Tricia crossed to the nearest table and needlessly adjusted the position of a gleaming silver dessert fork against the pristine white linen cloth covering the table. "I'm afraid my brother didn't give me much time to pull things together."

Lisa started. "*You* did all of this?" She assumed that Rourke had simply thrown enough money at the situation to make things turn around on his dime-size schedule.

Tricia nodded. "Do you like? I wasn't sure about the color, but Rourkey said you were wearing purple the first night he saw you."

Lisa's capacity for speech deserted her. Whether because of hearing him called *Rourkey,* or that he'd remembered what she was wearing that night in Shots all those months ago.

Seeming to notice her muteness, Sara Beth squeezed her hand. "It's all so beautiful," she answered into the silence.

Tricia smiled, obviously pleased. "Wait until you see the cake that Raoul's wife made. It's a thing of beauty." She leaned forward suddenly and gave Lisa a quick hug. "And before everything gets too crazy, welcome to the family."

Thoroughly discomfited, Lisa hugged her back. "Thank you." But as she straightened, she spotted Rourke, who'd arrived, seeming to bring up the tail end of their modest gathering of guests.

Fortunately for Lisa, Tricia immediately slid into general mode at the sight of her brother, and she simply went where she was directed—namely to one of the chairs at the center of the long tables.

It was easier than having to think, particularly when she was already consumed with the effort of maintaining a smiling facade in the face of all the good wishes that heaped upon her head.

Hardest, though, was when Nina Devlin—clearly fighting tears—was the last to offer a toast to their marriage. "It just took falling for the right girl to get my son properly down the aisle. I couldn't be happier to have such a beautiful girl as a new daughter." She sniffed and lifted her glass, her damp eyes looking right into Lisa's. "To you and my son. Take care of the love you have found. Take care of each other." She grinned suddenly. "And take care of the grandbabies I'm hoping you're not going to wait too long to give me!"

Laughter rounded the table as glasses softly clinked yet again and the breeze whispered around their heads, making the purple flowers marching down the centers of the tables dance.

It would all have been perfect.

If it had been real.

Rourke leaned close to her, his lips grazing her cheek. "Drink, for God's sake." His voice was soft, for her ears alone.

She smiled brightly and drank.

She turned her lips toward him for a glancing kiss whenever one of his sister's mischievous kids tapped their water glasses with a spoon. She pushed a few bites of Raoul's excellent food into her mouth when it seemed expected. She stood in front of the beautiful confection of a cake that Raoul wheeled out to cut the first slice to share with Rourke. She went through the motions with a smile on her face until she wanted to scream. But she didn't drop that smile until hours later, when the last guest had finally departed and even Raoul and his son, Tonio, and daughter, Maria, had left through a separate entrance off the kitchen that Lisa had yet to even see.

Only then, when it was just Rourke and Lisa left in that high-ceilinged living room scented by irises and filled with the soft sounds of a low guitar, did she finally, finally let the smile fade.

Her cheeks actually hurt.

She pulled off the fine shrug that matched her gown and dropped it on the end of one of the couches before sitting down to peel her feet out of the strappy designer torture devices otherwise known as sandals and wriggled her toes.

"Everyone seemed to enjoy themselves." Rourke slid off his jacket and tossed it next to her.

She automatically reached for it, her fingers smoothing out the finely pinstriped charcoal over the back of the couch so it wouldn't wrinkle. "Everyone but us."

His smile was faint. He pulled on his tie. "I wouldn't have minded everyone leaving an hour sooner than they did, but I thought it was okay. Food was good."

She realized she was staring at his strong throat where his fingers were loosening the collar of his shirt and quickly looked away. "Raoul doesn't disappoint." Though she would have been hard-pressed to remember what the menu had been.

She pushed to her feet only to nearly trip over her gown when she walked toward the windows. She lifted her skirts. "This is quite a view you have here. The skyline. The park."

"It's a place to sleep."

She made a soft sound. How easily he dismissed the million-dollar view. "Right." Her fingers toyed nervously with the diamond hanging just below her throat. The necklace had been a gift from her father when she'd graduated from college. Aside from Rourke's rings, it was the only other piece of jewelry that she was wearing. From the corner of her eye she saw him toss his tie aside as cavalierly as he had his jacket.

It made her even more acutely aware of how alone they were.

"That was, um, nice news Chance shared before they left," she said, feeling a little desperate. "About him adopting Jenny's daughter, Annie." Not until she'd seen Rourke slapping Chance on the back and kissing Jenny's face had she realized he was almost as good a friend with Chance as he was with Ted. She was still wearing her veil and the whisper-light silk tulle tickled her back. She reached back to unfasten it. "She's a sweetie."

"Yeah, she is. Chance'll be a good dad. He and Jenny are great together. Here. Let me."

A sharp wave of unease rolled through her. She sternly dismissed it. Theirs was a marriage of convenience. It didn't involve sex. Just because *she* couldn't get her mind off it didn't mean a thing.

She swallowed and turned her back toward him. "It's got more pins in it than you'd think," she warned.

"I'll find them." His fingers grazed against her head.

She closed her eyes, trying not to jump like some virgin on her wedding night.

It was almost laughable.

She wasn't a virgin, though she might as well have been for all of the experience she didn't really have.

And it was her wedding night.

But for them, those two things were not even relevant. It wasn't as if they'd need to sleep together to make a baby. They had the institute for that.

With surprising gentleness, he worked the handful of pins free, then unfastened the jeweled clasp of the veil and handed it over her shoulder to her. His bare forearm brushed against her.

When had he rolled up his shirtsleeves?

Feeling treacherously close to the edge of hysteria, she took the veil and quickly stepped away. "Bath and a bed," she blurted, only to feel her cheeks turn hot. "That's, um, that's what I think I need." She waved her hand, which also managed to wave the floating, silky veil. "Just point the way. I'll find it."

He looked amused. "Bedroom's down that hall."

"Great." She took a step only to tangle her bare foot in her skirt again. She hauled everything up in her arm. "Um… thanks." Her cheeks went even hotter. She was acting like an absolute idiot and knew it and before she made a bigger spectacle out of herself, she nearly ran down the hall. She found the bedroom with no difficulty, and closed herself behind the door with relief.

The furnishings there were just as sleekly designed, with a mile-wide pedestal bed and nightstands that seemed to grow right out of the wall on either side of it. There were acres of unused space, yet the room didn't feel stark or barren. Maybe because of the large fireplace that was opposite the bed, or the expanse of windows—again unadorned—that lined one wall.

Behind one of the doors the room possessed, she found her suitcase sitting on a luggage rack in the sizable closet. The closet then led to the en suite bathroom that, even in her exhausted state, was enough to make her swoon a little.

She flipped on the water over the massive tub and tossed in a generous measure of amber-colored salt from one of the heavy crystal containers decorating one corner of the stone ledge surrounding it. Immediately, lush, fragrant bubbles began to bloom beneath the rush of water and she reached for the buttons on the back of her dress only to realize with chagrin that there was no way that she would be able to undo enough of them on her own to even get the gown past her hips. Not even sliding her shoulders out of the narrow, fancily knotted chiffon that served as straps helped.

"Great." She eyed herself in the reflection of the wood-framed mirror that hung above the rectangular-shaped vessel sink. Her eyes looked wild and, thanks to pulling the pins from her veil loose, her hair was falling down.

"Lisa?"

She jerked, staring at a second door that led into the bathroom as it slowly opened. "What?"

Rourke stuck his head through. "I figured you'd need help with the dress."

She hated, absolutely hated, the fact that he'd realized that problem, too. But she walked over to him, presenting him with her back. "I do."

"Not the first time you've said those words today." His fingers grazed her back between her shoulder blades.

"Not the first time I didn't want to say those words today, either," she pointed out coolly. "Just get on with it." She pressed her hand against the bodice of the dress to hold it in place against her breasts as, centimeter by centimeter, she felt it loosening at the back.

"You know that telling me something like that just makes me want to take my time, right?"

She ignored him. It wasn't so easy, however, to ignore the feel of his fingers moving against her back. Even with the corset she wore beneath the gown, every grazing touch left her feeling branded.

She nearly laughed. Branded by his touch and shackled by his wedding ring.

He'd reached her waist. Another inch and she would be free of the dress, and of him. And, please God, the disturbing sensations roiling around inside her.

She held her breath, waiting. And the second she felt that bit of release, she started to step away.

But Rourke's hand slid right beneath the fabric of her gown, circling her waist. His palm pressed flat against the satin covering her belly as he tugged her back against him. "I've been wondering what was under the gown."

She could feel his shirt fabric against her shoulder blades. It was maddening. But what was more maddening was her weak longing to lean against the hard muscles she could feel beneath that shirt. "I *beg* your pardon?"

He laughed softly. "Let go of the dress." He didn't wait, but tugged the bodice out of her lamentably lax grip.

The gown slid to a fluffy cloud around her ankles, leaving her standing there wearing nothing but the white satin and lace corset and matching thong. And his hands.

Her frantic gaze landed on their reflection in the mirror, only to get caught in the snare of his gaze.

Never looking away from her, he lowered his head and pressed his mouth to the nape of her neck.

She swayed. His fingers splayed wider against her. Thumbs brushing against her corset-contained breasts. Little fingers sliding against the thin elastic of her insubstantial panties.

Desire wrenched through her, hot and wet and aching.

She drew in a hard, quick breath. She pushed away his hands and stepped out of the cloud to snatch it up against her. "This isn't part of the deal. I'm not…I'm not h-having sex with you!"

He tilted his head slightly, his eyes narrowing. "We're married now, Lisa *Devlin*. So tell me. What the hell do you think *is* the deal?"

Chapter Six

Lisa stared at Rourke. "Do we have to rehash it all? You want a child. I want to keep the institute from closing its doors." She lifted her hands. "And here we are."

He watched her for a tight, seemingly endless moment. "My child isn't going to be conceived in a petri dish."

Her stomach tightened. She advanced on him. "And just what is *that* supposed to mean?"

He had the gall to laugh. "I know you're not that naive."

She jabbed her finger against his chest. "I am *not* sleeping with you."

He grabbed her hand, holding it aloft so that her rings winked in the light, sending prisms around the room. "It's too late for reneging now. You agreed."

"I agreed to be a surrogate for you. I didn't agree to be your whore!"

"You agreed to be my wife." His voice turned as flat as his

eyes had gone. "To bear me a child. I never once said it would be the product of in vitro. And make no mistake. If I was going to treat you like a whore, I would've just taken you the night of the Founder's Ball and left the money on your nightstand."

"I don't know what infuriates me more." She finally managed to snatch her hand away from his hard grip. "Your absolute arrogance in thinking I would have slept with you that night, after sharing one dance with you, or you pretending now that this is what I agreed to! The Armstrong Institute specializes in IVF!"

"I didn't *marry* the Armstrong Institute!" His voice rose. He inhaled sharply. Let it out more slowly. "Obviously—" his voice was more controlled, even if his teeth were bared "—we're at cross-purposes, here." He suddenly moved, making her jump.

But he only moved past her to turn off the gushing water taps. "We'll conceive the baby in the normal way. I never said—or implied—otherwise."

She crossed her arms over the crumpled bodice of her dress, trying not to tremble.

She failed miserably.

"You know I *believed* otherwise." Her voice was stiff.

He lifted a sardonic brow. "Do I?"

She racked her brain. Surely they'd covered this. Hadn't they?

But the sinking sensation in her belly gave leeway for doubt to creep in.

She'd assumed.

And now, faced with his implacable certainty, she realized how badly she'd erred.

He did expect to sleep with her. To conceive a child, just as nature intended. And she…heaven help her…she had agreed to his terms without ever clarifying this most salient point.

"Rourke—" She barely managed to voice his name. "Honestly, we barely know each other. I didn't…I mean, I don't—"

"Save it." He lifted a weary hand. Ran it down his face. "You and I both know it doesn't matter *how* long we've known each other. It's enough. But it's been a long day. So take your bath."

She swallowed hard and couldn't prevent slanting a gaze toward the door through which he'd entered. Did it lead to his bedroom?

To his bed?

"And…and then?"

His black gaze raked over her. "Don't worry, princess. The mood's definitely passed for now."

She wanted to sag with relief but pride kept her shoulders more or less straight.

"Our flight leaves tomorrow morning." He went to the door. "But make no mistake, Lisa. Once we're in France on our *honeymoon*—" his lips twisted "—I expect to make this marriage a real one. I suggest you spend the time between now and then getting accustomed to the idea."

Then he left, closing the door softly, but finally, behind him.

She sank down on the wide ledge of the bubble-filled tub, her fingers still clutching the fabric of her wedding gown.

She was shaking. And she very much feared that it wasn't horror over her mammoth-size misunderstanding where her wifely duties were concerned.

It was anticipation.

And where was that going to leave her, once her purpose had been served?

The answer to that question was still eluding her when they boarded Rourke's private jet the following morning. And when they landed in Nice that night.

Rourke was no particular help. Aside from introducing her to his flight crew when they'd boarded the plane, he barely spoke to her once they were in the air.

Mostly, he spent the time on the phone. And most of that time he spent pacing the confines of the luxuriously equipped airplane. The only time he sat down in one of the sinfully soft leather seats was when Janine or Sandy, his two flight attendants, served them their meals.

She could almost have let herself believe that what had happened in his apartment the night before had never happened at all.

Almost.

Instead, her traitorous eyes kept tracking his movements about the cabin, willfully taking note of the sinuous play of muscles beneath his black trousers as he paced, of the way his hands gestured as he spoke, tendons standing out in his wrists where he'd rolled up the sleeves of his black shirt shortly after takeoff.

Now, they were gliding silently through a star-studded night as they left the airport behind in a low-slung sports car that offered very little space between her and Rourke, at the wheel.

There was no driver. No flight crew.

Just…the two of them.

And all too easily, her senses were filled with the memory of his lips brushing against the nape of her neck, his hands sliding over her.

In the faint glow of the dashboard lights, she could see that hand capably curled over the steering wheel.

She bit her lip for a long moment and opened her window a few inches to let in the rush of night air but it wasn't anywhere near cool enough to suit her.

"You all right?"

"Just a little tired." It wasn't entirely a lie. Despite traveling in the cradle of luxury, the flight had still taken hours. Add in the time difference and it meant it was nearly midnight there. "I thought it would be cooler outside."

"Weather around here is pretty temperate year-round and August wasn't long ago. There's still heat lingering. Might even find the water still good for swimming." He glanced at her, then back at the road. "We'll be on a private beach."

She lowered the window another few inches, wanting the wind to blow away the ideas *that* caused.

The road they were driving on was narrow. Winding and, aside from the gleam of moonlight, very, very dark. They might have been the only two people left in the world.

"My father took me to Paris once," she desperately interrupted the insistent images filling her head. "I was still in college." It was the first time he'd included her in such a manner and she'd been thrilled to accompany him to the medical conference. "But we were so busy that I never had a chance to leave the city."

"Busy doing what?"

She was vaguely surprised that he even responded. It seemed unlikely that he was as tensely nervous as she. But still, conversation was better than silence, and it might keep her imagination under some control. "Keeping up with my father, mostly. He was presenting some new research at a conference." She thought back, remembering. "He was amazing."

She hadn't been offended to be the one fetching him water or carrying his papers. And when he'd included her in his conversations—had actually seemed proud of her when she'd offered some thought or opinion—she'd felt as if she'd accomplished something truly great. "It was the first time he actually treated me like an adult."

She felt Rourke's glance, but he didn't comment as he slowed the car to turn up a steep drive that seemed to appear out of nowhere. A dimly lit gate swung open for them, and once they were through, the road became even more winding and narrow.

Yet he navigated it all with obvious ease.

"I take it you've been here before."

"Mmm."

She chewed the inside of her lip. "With a woman?" She hated acknowledging the need to know.

His hesitation was barely noticeable. "None I've been married to."

She couldn't tell if it was amusement in his voice or irony.

But there was no time to dwell too long on wondering what woman—or women—had been here with him, because he pulled to a stop in a small stone-paved courtyard. "This is it."

There was not much to see beyond the low lights that were bright enough only to point out the perimeter of the courtyard and light the way along a narrow walkway. She climbed out of the car while he was pulling their suitcases out of the trunk that had probably taken some mathematical genius to fit inside in the first place, and even though she held out her hand to take some of her own smaller items, he just ignored her and loaded the straps up on his own muscular shoulders.

She wouldn't have thought the man would ever carry his own luggage.

"This way." He headed toward the walkway. "Watch your step. The lighting is pretty dim and the pavers might be uneven."

As she followed him, she also noticed that the bushes lining the walk were overgrown, which didn't help the going any. She was glad she was wearing flats, though her gauzy ankle-length skirt wanted to snag against the overgrowth. Before long, they passed through an archway that led into another courtyard and he unlocked a wide, tall door, and led her inside.

Given his taste in homes, she shouldn't have been surprised by the luxury that met them when he began flipping on lights as they passed through the entrance hall to a living area that rivaled his New York apartment for size. But after the rustic entryway, nevertheless, she was.

In his apartment, everything had seemed angular. Here, everything was arched—the doorways that were flanked by marble columns and the windows that were covered with shutters. The floors were gleaming stone and the furnishings all seemed to be done in soft browns. It was cool and elegant and expensively beautiful and she couldn't help but wonder if the paintings that hung on the smooth, ivory walls were originals.

He dumped their luggage on the floor and crossed the long room to push open the shutters guarding the tall arch-shaped windows there. "I told Marta—the housekeeper—that we wouldn't need her until tomorrow." Lisa realized they weren't windows at all but doors, when he pulled them right open letting in the fresh night air. "Come out and see the view."

Nerves jumping anew, she followed him outside onto a deep terrace guarded by a majestic stone balustrade that faithfully followed the steps that crisscrossed from this level to two lower ones, and finally the ghostly white sand that led to the silver-white glisten of the sea. "It's breathtaking," she admitted.

"Wait until you see it at sunrise."

"Sunrise?" She shook her head. "Thank you, no. I prefer to be sleeping at that hour."

His white teeth flashed in a quick grin that caused her heart to smack around even more than the view had. "Some things are worth getting up for at that hour."

She couldn't form a response to that to save her soul.

And he knew it.

His grin deepened as he turned to go back inside. "I'll show you the rest of the place."

Aside from the main living area, "the place" included two kitchens, one media room, an office that Rourke said was equipped with every convenience, and a total of six bedrooms.

"This one has the best view," he said of the very last one they came to.

And she could certainly see why.

The wide four-poster bed was positioned opposite a bank of windows that he immediately set about un-shuttering. They'd gone down a short flight of stairs to reach the room and it looked out the same direction as the living room, sharing that stellar view of the Mediterranean.

It didn't take a genius to realize *this* was the room he was expecting they would share. The room. And the bed.

She kept her eyes strictly away from that particular item and went into the adjoining bathroom. Even that had windows that opened up to the view.

She pressed her palm to the knots in her belly and returned to the bedroom.

Rourke, done with the windows at last, watched her for a moment. "Marta will unpack everything in the morning. Do you want one of those suitcases for tonight?"

She hadn't considered herself a normal bride. She hadn't packed a trousseau. No sexy little negligees designed strictly for the purpose of enticing an eager groom. No fancy little ensembles to parade around in during the day. She'd packed what she'd had in her closet.

The only thing new that she'd worn in the past two days had been her wedding gown.

And everything beneath it.

Her mind shied away from those thoughts.

"I just need the overnighter. The small one. But I can get it…" She was already speaking to an empty room and could hear the sound of his footsteps on the half-dozen stairs that would carry him back to the living room's level.

She let out a shaking breath, looking around the room again. The bathroom had possessed several mirrors, but the bedroom itself contained none and for that she was grateful. There were two large armoires on each side of the room and a bureau in the arching hallway that opened into the adjacent bathroom. She peeked inside each, finding them all empty.

Rourke still hadn't returned, so she opened one of the French doors and went outside onto the terrace.

If she looked up and to her right, she could see the terrace level off the living room. If she looked down and to her left, she could see the lowest terrace, which could be reached by another set of stairs. But the terrace on which she stood was the only one that possessed a setting of deeply cushioned chaises and chairs positioned beneath a tall pergola. Long, pale drapes hung down the colonnades, drifting softly in the night air.

She couldn't help the sigh that escaped. It was all so impossibly beautiful.

If he chose a place like this for a honeymoon with someone he didn't remotely love, what would he do for someone he did?

"Here."

She whirled on her heel, pushing aside the disturbing thought. What did she care what he'd do for someone he loved?

Rourke stood in the deep shadow of the doorway, holding out her small case. She went to him and carefully lifted the strap away from his hand before sidling past him into the room.

Now what?

She was so far out of her element she didn't have a clue. She twisted the leather strap in her hands. "I—"

"I—"

They both broke off.

He lifted an eyebrow, but she just shook her head, mute all over again.

"I have some calls to make."

It was the last thing she expected him to say. "It's the middle of the night."

"Not in New York." He started to leave the room again. "It's going to take me at least a few hours so if you're hungry, I'm sure you can find something in the kitchen."

"I don't cook."

He glanced back at her. "Don't, or don't know how?"

Her cheeks went hot. "Does it matter?"

He shrugged and she felt positive it was her fanciful imagination that colored his faint smile with a shade of indulgence. "Cooking isn't part of the job description. But this place is always stocked with fruit and breads. Even someone who doesn't cook won't starve."

Job description.

Her hands curled so tightly, the leather strap dug into her palms. "I suppose *you* want something to eat."

His eyes were unreadable. "I'll manage."

Then he turned and left her alone and she almost wished she had jumped on the idea of preparing them some sort of meal. Because now all she was left with was that wide bed behind her and the sense that she was expected to prepare herself for it.

And for him.

Nerves spurred her into motion and she dumped her overnighter on the bureau. She needed to stop thinking like some Victorian virgin. She was a modern twenty-first-century woman, for God's sake.

She yanked open the case and unloaded the few items inside. The travel bag containing her toiletries, the oversize Bruins jersey that she preferred to sleep in, and a pair of clean, thoroughly utilitarian white cotton panties.

Not a speck of lace or ribbon or silk in sight.

Sadly, she didn't know if she'd have felt more confident if there had been. Probably not.

She was far more comfortable in a suit sitting in a boardroom debating business practices than she was in a nightgown waiting for a man….

She had a few hours, according to what he'd said, but instead of attempting another bath when the memory of her last attempt was so fresh in her mind, she unpinned her hair and took a short, steaming shower and tried not to think about the fact that the slate-tiled enclosure was certainly roomy enough for two.

When she got out, she wrapped her wet hair in one of the plentiful plush terry towels, slathered lotion on her arms and legs—just like she did every time she showered, she justified—pulled on the jersey and bikini pants, and, feeling like a thief in the night, crept her way through the villa to the nearest kitchen. There was, indeed, a wide assortment of foods already available.

She selected a crusty roll and a handful of green grapes and turned to go back to the bedroom. But the chilled bottle of wine that had already been opened caught her eye, and she grabbed that, too, as well as one of the wineglasses that hung from beneath one of the whitewashed cupboards. Feeling even more thieflike, she stole back to the bedroom, carefully skirting around the office.

But her footsteps dragged to a halt when the low murmur of Rourke's voice through the partially closed door shaped into distinguishable words. "Call the publisher," he was saying. "Tell him if he doesn't squash the story, I'll personally call on every corporate advertiser they've got and he won't like the results."

One of the grapes rolled out of Lisa's hand and she silently darted after it, catching it just before it rolled down one of the steps.

She looked back and saw Rourke watching her, his phone still at his ear.

She flushed a little. "I was hungry after all."

His gaze settled on the wine bottle, looking amused. "And thirsty?"

"This *is* France. And the bottle was already opened."

"You don't have to defend yourself to me." He abruptly turned his attention back to the phone. "You're damn right I'm serious." His voice was sharp, obviously intended for his caller. "If you can't accomplish this, I'll hire someone who can." He went back into the office, closing the door behind him.

Lisa scurried down the steps to the bedroom feeling a little sorry for whomever was on the other end of that call.

She quickly demolished the bread and grapes even before she finished half a glass of wine. She pulled out her own cell phone and started to dial Sara Beth twice.

But she didn't want to burden her friend with foolishly panicked calls. Aside from Rourke's insistence that nobody know the true details of their agreement, Sara Beth's new husband was Rourke's friend and Lisa was loath to put her problems between them. Particularly when Lisa suspected that Sara Beth was already concerned.

So she put the phone away.

She paced around the bed, avoiding it as if it was poisonous, until finally, annoyed with herself, she yanked back the creamy silk bedspread and bunched up a few of the bed pillows behind her back. She pulled out the suspense novel that she'd brought with her, but reading it now was just as big a pretense as it had been on the plane, and she finally tossed it aside.

A part of her wished Rourke would just return and put an end to this painful waiting, once and for all.

But he didn't return. And the time display on her cell phone told her that not even an hour had passed, anyway.

She got out of bed, grabbed the bedspread off the bed and carried it, along with her wine, out onto the terrace. There, she wrapped the bedspread around her and stretched out on one of the chaises to stare into the dark, gleaming mystery of the Mediterranean sea. And there, finally, for the first time since she'd met Rourke in Raoul's restaurant, she felt herself begin to relax.

She never noticed when Rourke eventually came to the door of the bedroom and looked out at her to find her head bundled in terry cloth towel and her body wrapped in silk.

Because she was fast asleep.

Rourke sighed faintly and picked up the wine bottle from the wrought-iron table beside her and gave it a shake. Empty. There was still a good measure of liquid left in her glass, though, and he finished it off.

Then he leaned over her and scooped her, bedspread and all, off the chaise.

The lopsided towel unwound from her head, falling to the ground and her long hair tumbled free, damp and tangled, against his shoulder. He went stock-still, though, when her nose found its way to the hollow of his throat and her hand slid over his shoulder.

"I hope you didn't fire the guy on the phone." She sighed so deeply he felt her warm breath on his throat and fast heat pooled low in his gut.

The last thing he wanted to think about was his conversation with his media director, who'd called to warn him that some reporter had been nosing around, tying together the co-incidence of Derek Armstrong's resignation as the institute's CFO with a reported sighting that he'd checked into an exclusive detox center in Connecticut on the very same day that his sister married Rourke. "I didn't fire him." He turned sideways to carry her into the bedroom and nudged the door shut behind them. Then he settled her on the mattress.

"'S good." She turned on her side, kicking at the confining bedspread until one long, slender leg was freed, then tucked her hands beneath her cheek.

He reached back to turn off the bedside lamp, plunging the room into darkness that was relieved only by the slant of moonlight through the windows. "Sleep tight, princess," he murmured and started to turn.

"Where're you going?" She pushed up on her elbow. Her wildly tangled hair streamed over one shoulder and the shirt she was wearing had slipped off the other.

To hell, he thought.

He reached for his belt and pulled it free. "Nowhere."

In the faint light, he could see her slowly close her eyes and she lowered her head again.

Even before he climbed into bed beside her minutes later, he knew she was once again fast asleep. He still scooped her against him. And when she didn't try to roll away, didn't do anything but offer a deep exhale that seemed to press her body more closely against him, he slowly pressed his lips to her fragrant hair and closed his eyes.

Who knew that hell could be so close to heaven?

Chapter Seven

It was the rattle of china that finally dragged Lisa out of the comforting oblivion of her warm cocoon.

She opened her eyes, squinting against the bright sunshine that filled the room, getting a glimpse of the deepest blue sky she'd ever seen through the windows, as well as the attractive brunette who was settling the tray on the nightstand beside Lisa's head.

"Monsieur Devlin said you might wish for some coffee," the girl said in heavily accented English.

Lisa nodded, only to wince at the dull pain that reverberated through her head at the motion. She pushed up onto her elbow, gingerly taking the cup and saucer that the girl had filled and was holding out to her. "Thank you. Are you Marta?"

"Mais non, madame. Je suis Sylvie." She quickly rounded the bed to the other side of Lisa and began straightening the pillows there, sweeping her hands deftly over the tumbled bedding.

Lisa eyed her, warily trying to see beyond the pain in her head to her memory of the night before. She'd eaten a little…Rourke had been on the phone…the wine…the chaise.

Her stomach clenched as she recalled the sensation of floating, his arms around her.

He'd obviously slept in the bed.

But had they done anything else?

Was it possible they'd made love and now she couldn't even remember it?

Feeling as if she'd fallen down the rabbit hole, she rubbed her hands over her eyes. Surely she'd remember…

"I can bring madame *les croissants et les fruits?*"

"No, thank you." She pushed the rattling cup and saucer onto the nightstand before she managed to spill the steaming brew all over herself and the bed, and sat up on the side of the mattress. "Can you tell me where Mr. Devlin is?"

The girl dimpled. "Swimming, madame. As he does every morning when he stays here."

Lisa pushed off the bed, yanking the hem of the jersey down around her thighs, and strode over to the French doors that were opened to the warmth of the morning sun. Ignoring the clanging inside her head at both the motions and the unrelenting sunlight, she went out onto the terrace and, sure enough, she could see Rourke's black head bobbing in the blue, blue sea.

"In case you wish to join him?" Sylvia appeared silently beside her bearing a plush white robe.

"I'm not exactly wearing a swimsuit."

The girl merely smiled. "Nor is he, madame."

Lisa snatched the robe and yanked it on, covering her jersey as well as her self-consciousness. "Thank you, Sylvie."

The girl tilted her head slightly, managing to look amused and sly at the same time, before she disappeared back into the house.

Maybe Rourke didn't need to *bring* women to this place if the lovely Sylvie was already at his beck and call.

Annoyed with herself for even wondering, she stomped barefoot down the steps to the lower terrace. Her feet met the coarse sand, slowing her speed considerably, but she made it to the towel that he'd dropped in a heap just beyond the water's reach.

He obviously knew she was there. He waved an arm, gesturing for her to come in.

In answer, she gathered the robe around her and sat down on top of his towel.

Despite the distance, she could see the flash of his teeth. Then his head disappeared beneath the surface of the glimmering water, reappearing again a moment later, considerably closer to shore. Before long, he was rising up altogether as he walked through the chest-high water as one hand slicked his hair back out of his face. Then the water was at his waist.

His hips.

She shaded her eyes, ostensibly from the sunlight, but just as much to hide the effort it took not to drop her jaw and just stare, when he kept right on coming. All warm, tanned flesh stretched over long, roping muscles.

Warm, naked flesh.

Not even being forewarned was enough to prepare her.

He walked right out of the sea like some pagan God with water streaming down his corrugated abdomen, his thighs. His…everything.

And he didn't stop until he was less than two feet away. "My towel," he finally prompted.

Flushing, caught staring, she shifted off the towel and practically threw it at him.

Not bothering to hide his smile, he easily caught it and ran it down his chest. She was almost pathetically grateful when he wrapped it around his hips because she wasn't sure she would ever regain the art of breathing if he didn't.

"I met Sylvie." It wasn't at all what she should be saying, much less in such a waspish tone.

"I told her to make sure you had coffee before noon. Figured you'd need it after last night." He stretched out on the sand beside her, his head propped on his hand. With his hair slicked back from his face, he looked even more devilish. Black eyes bright, thick lashes clinging together with sparkling water drops, the whisper of a sardonic grin hovering around his mobile lips.

"Is *she* one of the women you've been here with?"

The slashing line beside his lips deepened. "She's a child."

"She didn't look very childish to me."

He tugged at her robe's belt until it came loose. "Mrs. Devlin, are you sounding jealous?"

"Certainly not. I just don't want to be embarrassed by coming face-to-face with one of my *husband's* lovers while on my honeymoon."

He gave a bark of laughter and captured her ankle in his hand. She nearly jumped out of her skin and wasn't helped any when his palm began slowly running up her calf beneath the loose folds of the robe. "Sylvie is Marta's niece," he drawled, his gaze capturing hers and allowing no escape. "Marta is a longtime employee of the owner, who happens to be a good friend of mine." His warm, still-wet palm reached her knee and began inching along the descent of her thigh. "And while we're married, the only lover I'll have is you."

She clamped her hand over his wrist, stopping the progress of his utterly distracting hand before it crept any farther toward the hem of her hockey jersey. "*Have?* Does that mean we already—last night—" She broke off, miserably humiliated at even having to ask.

His eyes were inscrutable. "You don't remember?"

Her jaw tightened. "Obviously. Not."

He moved suddenly, and instead of her hand capturing his wrist, he'd pushed her down and pressed hers into the sand above her head while he settled over her. "Princess, you'll definitely know when it's the morning after."

She drew in a shuddering breath, excruciatingly aware of every solid, male inch pressed against her from breast to toe. "Then w-we didn't."

He lowered his head until his lips were a hairsbreadth from hers. "We did not," he said softly. Slowly.

She swallowed and a soft sound rose in her throat that was either acknowledgment or relief or despair. She wasn't sure and, at that moment, wasn't sure that she cared.

He ran his other hand down the side of her head, threading through the tangles in her hair. "And when we do, it's not going to be because you're down half a bottle of wine just so you can face being in my bed."

"There wasn't even enough left in that bottle for two glasses."

"And you have no head for even one," he pointed out softly. "I saw that the first day at Fare. But you're clearheaded now, aren't you." His lips slowly settled against hers; not exactly a kiss, not exactly *not* a kiss.

Whatever it was, it made her forget the dull throb behind her eyes.

It left her heart charging inside her chest.

It had her fingers curling and uncurling against the sand.

"It's broad daylight." Her lips moved against his, her whisper barely audible. "Anyone could see us."

He angled his head finally, moving until his lips tickled the lobe of her ear. "Private beach. Nobody's watching." His hand left her hair and slid over her throat, working the lapels of the terry cloth robe out from between them.

"But Sylvie. Marta."

"Know better than to look," he assured her. "And if they do, what will they see?" His hands slid beneath the jersey, drawing it up her hip and stealing her breath. "A husband and wife on their honeymoon."

She sank her teeth into her tongue when his fingers grazed the flat of her stomach, but a sound still escaped. And then he was moving again, his weight leaving her, only she was still pinned against the sand by the ungodly pleasure of his mouth pressing against her navel.

"Wait," she gasped, wrenching her wrists free from his grip to press her hands against his shoulders.

He barely lifted his head. His gleaming eyes looked at her. "For what?" Watching her steadily, he pressed his lips against her abdomen.

Her muscles jumped. She sucked in a breath. "I—" She had no answer. What *were* they waiting for?

Her nerve?

His lips inched higher. Pressed another kiss. Still he watched her.

His gaze was equally as disturbing as the feel of his lips, warm and surprisingly soft, particularly compared to the tingling abrasion of his unshaven jaw against her belly.

He nudged the jersey fabric higher, followed by another kiss.

Nudged again, nearly over her breasts. She felt the breath of balmy air against skin that had never directly felt it. "I don't do this," she said faintly. "Roll around naked on the beach like in some movie scene."

"You're not really naked," he murmured. With excruciating slowness, he dragged the jersey against her agonizingly tight nipples until they sprang free. "Not yet."

Her lips parted, searching for breath that wouldn't come. Her heart raced dizzily. His gaze finally left hers to survey what he'd revealed.

His fingers balled the fabric in his fist. "Beautiful." His voice was low. Rough.

His head dipped again to taste, and her back bowed off the sand at the feel of his mouth capturing first one hard, tight peak, then the other. She felt drenched in fire. "Rourke—" She couldn't take it. "Please."

"That's the plan. Please you." He kissed his way up the slope of her breast. "Please me."

"No." She was shaking her head, even as he was pulling the oversize jersey over it. "I can't. Not like this." But her heels were dragging into the sand while her knees lifted and her traitorous thighs hugged his.

"Can't, or won't?" He braced himself on his arms, keeping from crushing her, but the dark swirl of hair on his chest was a crisp tickle against her breasts. His narrowed eyes searched hers.

She could feel him hard and heavy and waiting. The only things separating them were a loosely draped towel and her panties, both of which could be so easily disposed of.

And heaven help her, but she wanted those barriers gone. She felt hollow and achingly wet and he was the means to heal her.

She'd never wanted anyone like this. She'd known it ever since that single, unforgettable turn around the dance floor with him at the Founder's Ball, even while he'd been making caustic comments about the fancy party that test-tube babies had paid for.

But none of that came to her lips as she stared mutely into his eyes.

She felt the push of his chest in the deep breath he drew. Her lips felt swollen and tingled when his gaze dropped to them. He ran his palm along her jaw, moved his thumb over her lower lip.

A small part of her brain warned her that she was only imagining a tenderness in his touch. A larger part of her body wanted to just sink into it.

His gaze lifted again and caught hers. "What are you afraid of?"

It was the last thing she expected from him. Cool irritation. Arrogant demand. Not this unexpected, unwanted softly voiced insight.

"Tell me." His voice dropped even lower.

"Everything." The admission was nearly as much a release as the one her body was aching for him to give her. Hot tears suddenly leaked from the corners of her eyes. "I'm afraid of everything," she whispered again. "Everything's out of control."

"Everything?"

"You," she amended huskily. "You make me feel out of control."

He didn't smile. Didn't gloat.

And it was more dangerous than if he had, because *that* she could have shored up her defenses against.

Instead, he simply asked softly, "What's safer than losing control in the arms of your husband?"

She couldn't bear the gentle probing in his eyes and closed hers. "Nothing if we were an ordinary couple. Which we're anything but."

He was silent for a moment. A moment filled with the lap of water, the whisper of a breeze, and the weight of this man whose words did nothing to allay the desire still holding her in its grip. "Control's important to you."

She let out a careful breath. "Isn't it to you?"

"I'm a man."

Her eyes flew open. She stared, then laughed brokenly. "Right. And for a man—particularly a man like you—your need to stay in control is acceptable and expected. But because I'm a woman—" She broke off, shaking her head.

He nudged her chin with his thumb until she was looking

at him again. "I know the reasons why I control the things I do. To achieve the things I want."

"And what you want now is a child. Which is the only reason you want me."

He shook his head slightly and smoothed his thumbs down the tracks of her tears. "That's not the only reason. I wanted you long before it occurred to me that we could help each other."

And it scared the living wits right out of her. Men like Rourke didn't want women like Lisa. They wanted beautiful, sexy, accomplished women. Women who were as comfortable in their bedrooms as they were in their offices.

"I told you it's all going to be all right." His mesmerizing gaze held hers even when he pressed his mouth against hers in a slow, drugging kiss that had her bones melting all over again.

And just when she was on the verge of collapsing into it, to twine her arms around his broad, broad shoulders, and pull him down onto her, into her, he suddenly jackknifed off her and grabbed her hands in his, hauling her up to her feet. "Come on."

She very nearly stumbled, taking a few steadying steps in the sand as he leaned down again to scoop up her jersey and his towel that had slipped free, giving her another heart-stopping view. He dropped the jersey back over her shoulders, slung the towel around his waist again, and shook the sand out of her robe before handing it to her.

Bemused, she took it and followed, unresisting, when he took her hand and led her back up the short stretch of sand to the stairs leading up to their bedroom terrace. Expecting him to lead her right to that big bed that they'd shared but hadn't "shared," confusion joined the miasma of emotions swirling inside her when he just let go of her hand once they were inside, and headed to the dressing room.

She looked from his departing backside to the bed that Sylvie must have finished making after Lisa had gone down to the beach, and back again. But Rourke didn't return and a moment later she heard the sound of the shower.

She shoved her hands through her hair, fingers catching in the tangles, as she pressed her palms against her head.

She did not understand the man she'd married at all.

Before she realized it, her feet had carried her into the spa-like bathroom where steam was already forming against the clear glass shower walls. The steam had not, unfortunately, begun to cloud the mirrors and before she could demand to know what game he was playing now, she caught a glimpse of her reflection.

She cringed, nearly groaning right out loud.

She looked like something the cat had dragged in. Hair sticking out at all angles. Day-old mascara smudging shadows around her eyes.

Ignoring the distraction of Rourke's movements behind the cloudy shower glass, she snatched open her cosmetic bag. She washed her face. Brushed her teeth. And was just beginning to attack the snarls in her hair when Rourke shut off the shower and stepped out, again displaying that singularly un-selfconscious demeanor as he stopped behind her, heedlessly dripping water everywhere as he slipped the comb out of her nerveless fingers.

She couldn't pretend that her face wasn't blushing fiery red, but she *could* ignore it. "The tangles will get worse if I don't get them out."

"Then sit." Rourke closed his hand over her shoulder when she stood there staring at him in the reflection of the mirror, and he nudged her toward the padded stool tucked beside the vanity.

Looking too surprised to protest, she sat and looked even more bemused when he stood behind her and lifted up the ends of her hair to start working the tangles free with the comb. "It's longer than I expected," he admitted.

Her brown eyes widened. "You thought about…my hair?" She sounded so disbelieving that he almost laughed.

At himself.

He'd thought about a lot more than her hair. And now she was his wife and he was no closer to having her than he'd ever been, because he'd realized that he couldn't force himself to force her to want him in return. "You always have it pulled up," he said.

She'd curled her hands together in her lap. Tightly. And was watching him in the mirror as if he were crazy. "What are you doing?"

Maybe he was crazy. His hands kept working, patiently making his way from the ends of her hair to the scalp. "Keeping you from ripping so much of your hair out that you're left half bald."

"Why?"

He nudged her head forward with a finger. "Because I want to. Blame it on my controlling nature."

She gave an exasperated humph. "Where'd you learn to comb out tangles?"

"My sisters are all younger than me," he reminded her. "Someone had to help my mother with them."

Her gaze caught his in the mirror and damned if he felt able to look away.

"I can't figure you out," she said softly.

She wasn't the only one. "I'm just a man." He finally, deliberately lowered his gaze back to her head. "I can ditch the towel if you need reminding."

She huffed softly again. "You could probably buy and sell small countries but you insisted on marrying me to keep your mother happy."

Not just his mother. He moved on to another satiny hank of tangled hair, not commenting.

"And here you are combing out my hair."

"That sounds more like an accusation than an observation." He draped the tangle-free length over her shoulder and moved to the next section. Her head tilted slightly, revealing that tantalizing little freckle.

His mouth felt dry. Here he was. Surrounded by the ocean of her while thirst was slowly, but surely killing him off.

"You're close to your sisters."

"Mmm-hmm." She was an observant woman and it wasn't something he'd tried to hide.

"They all have children. Are you just trying to keep up with them?"

His lips twisted. Not with amusement. "I want kids. Not so unusual. Haven't you thought about having them?"

"Not until you forced me to think about it," she returned. "Now, I feel constantly confronted by it."

He didn't reply to that. He merely stroked the comb one last time through her waving hair that was now free of knots, and then handed it to her. "Get dressed. We'll go into town for lunch."

He left the bathroom and Lisa turned on her stool to watch him go to one of the armoires in the bedroom and pull out a lightweight shirt and pants. He was nearly fully dressed and she was *still* sitting there, trying to understand the odd progression of the day.

Trying to understand this man to whom she was now married.

Finally, he stopped in the middle of the bedroom. His white linen shirt was untucked over beige pants. With his black hair still damp and tousled and his unshaven jaw shadowed, he looked expensively casual—and seriously sexy.

And a large part of her was demanding to know why she'd had to go and ruin what had started on the beach.

"I don't understand you at all," she admitted, beyond caring at that point what sort of edge she was probably allowing him.

"What's to understand? I'm hungry." He pushed his feet into leather loafers, missing the face she made.

"I wasn't talking about the lunch plans." Which she knew he was well aware even before he straightened again with the faint smile back on his face.

"You need to stop thinking so much," he said.

"If I could stop thinking, we'd have been having sex down there on the beach." She flushed all over again.

His eyebrows lifted a little. He gestured toward the opened doors leading to the terrace. "Then we'll go back down there. We can always have lunch later—"

"No." She quickly pushed to her feet. She was afraid he was playing with her, but that didn't mean she trusted him not to put words to action.

She knew that the time would come—sooner rather than later—when she'd have to live up to her end of the bargain. He'd bought his way into her uterus, in exchange for saving that which mattered most to her. The institute.

But that didn't mean she was ready yet to face the fact that in the process, she'd also sold him a place in her bed.

"I have sand on my legs," she said, reaching for the door between them. "I need a shower before I dress." Before he could comment, she closed the door.

It wasn't a significant exercise of control, but it was better than nothing.

And when it came to Rourke, she needed every speck she could hoard.

Chapter Eight

Once Lisa was showered and dressed in a strapless yellow sundress with her hair pulled back again in its customary—and safely familiar—knot, they drove down to the village and left the car parked in a picturesque cobblestone alleyway bordered by ageless stone buildings graced with iron railings and colorful flowerboxes and walked to the nearby open-air market. Rourke seemed very familiar with the merchants that they passed, smiling and laughing off comments with ease that her long-ago high-school French couldn't hope to keep up with.

She found she didn't much care, though, because she was too busy taking in the incredible sights that the tiny seaside town had to offer and then Rourke was guiding her to a collection of unoccupied tables situated next to a small building. As soon as she'd taken the sun-bleached chair that he held out for her, a wizened old man came out of the building, his arms outstretched in greeting. "Rourke," he called, smiling broadly. "Who iz zis beautiful woman you bring to me?"

Rourke closed his hand over her shoulder. "Tyrus, this is my wife, Lisa. We married a few days ago."

"Marriage?" Tyrus's wiry eyebrows shot up over his buttonlike eyes and then he grabbed up Lisa's hand, bowing low over it. *"Très belle."*

Too aware of the warm hand that felt wholly possessive on her bare shoulder, Lisa barely noticed the kiss that Tyrus bestowed on the back of her hand. "It's nice to meet you," she managed when the diminutive man had straightened again.

"Oui, oui." He was nodding over and over again. "I bring you wine," he announced suddenly, turning on his heel to hurry back to the building. "We celebrate!"

Rourke pulled out the chair next to her and sat down. Their knees brushed beneath the little round iron table and though her instinct was to shift her legs, she resisted, mostly because of the gleam in his eyes that told her that was exactly what he expected her to do. "Obviously people know you in the village, too," she said.

"I've been coming here for a lot of years." Looking idle, he threaded his fingers through hers and his platinum wedding band gleamed in the sunlight.

For some reason, she found herself feeling mesmerized by the sight and deliberately blinked, focusing instead on the prolific red blooms of the lush bougainvillea that grew against the whitewashed walls of the building next to their table.

"Something wrong?"

She shook her head. "What brought you here in the first place?"

"An old friend."

"The same friend who owns the villa?"

"Yes."

Her teeth worried the inside of her upper lip. "A woman?"

His thumb slid in slow circles over hers. "I think you *do* have a jealous streak."

"Not in this lifetime," she lied coolly.

"Here we are," Tyrus reappeared, holding a bottle and several glasses aloft.

"We need some lunch, too," Rourke advised, sitting back in his chair. "I figured we'd see Grif and Nora here already."

"They still come every afternoon," Tyrus assured him as he deftly poured the deep red wine and even before he'd finished, a shapely blonde girl appeared with a tray that she sat on a neighboring table before tossing her arms around Rourke's shoulder to give him a long kiss right on the lips.

Lisa's jaw tightened and she pulled her hand out of Rourke's. He didn't protest. But then how could he?

He had his arms full of French blonde who was all but sitting on his lap.

"Rourke?" Another voice interrupted them, and Lisa looked up to see an older couple crossing the narrow street toward them.

With a deep chuckle, Rourke finally set aside the pouting blonde. "Lisa, Martine," he introduced carelessly as she rose.

"Old *friends?*" Lisa lifted her eyebrows. Rourke laughed, which was no answer at all, but Lisa was glad to see the blonde move away and disappear into the small building. Tyrus just stood by, beaming.

"I thought that was you." The woman, gray-haired, chicly styled and with no hint of a French accent, reached them and took the hands Rourke held out, and lifted her cheeks for his kiss. "Why didn't you tell us you were coming?"

Lisa saw the look that passed between Rourke and the man accompanying her.

"He did, darling." The man, tall and balding, slid his arm

over the woman's slender shoulders as he shook Rourke's hand. "I told you last week that he was coming to use the villa."

The woman frowned a little, then shrugged with a little laugh. "My memory," she dismissed and focused on Lisa. "Are you a friend of Rourke's?"

Lisa was getting the impression that Rourke had plenty of "friends" in this part of the world.

"You would be Rourke's Lisa," the man answered even before Rourke or Lisa could. He rounded the small table and took Lisa's hand in both of his. Kindness shined out of his bright blue eyes. "He's told us so much about you. I'm Griffin Harper," the man said to her. "And Rourke's not actually family, but Nora and I feel like he is, so I'm still going to say welcome to the family." He leaned over and kissed Lisa's cheek, giving her no room whatsoever for feeling awkward.

"Of course!" The woman—Nora—clasped her hands together. "How could I forget? You got married again." She darted around the table and enveloped Lisa in a quick, Chanel-scented hug. "If we'd have had more notice, we'd have come to New York for the ceremony. Honestly, I never thought he'd get over that unfortunate business with Taylor," she whispered.

Feeling more than a little bewildered, and definitely self-conscious being at the center of this attention, Lisa looked to Rourke. He obviously hadn't heard Nora's comment, since he and Griffin were busy pulling a second table and chairs closer.

Martine appeared with more glasses, which Tyrus quickly filled before he lifted his own in a toast. *"Pour l'amour."*

"For love," Griffin repeated, smiling benevolently.

The fondness they all felt for Rourke was plainly evident and even though she felt a fraud, Lisa managed to smile and drink and even to eat the excellent bread and cheese that Rourke broke off and fed to her.

The attention he gave her clearly delighted his friends, but she wasn't so easily fooled.

He was doing it to get under her skin.

And unfortunately, was being all too successful at it.

Then, when he whisked her partially finished glass of wine away from her to replace it with a bottle of sparkling water, Nora gave a little gasp. "You're not drinking. Are you pregnant?"

The lively chatter gave way to dead silence as everyone turned their attention to Lisa and she felt heat creep up her cheeks. She wanted to crawl under the table and hide. "No—"

"Not yet," Rourke inserted. He lifted her hand, watching her boldly as he kissed her knuckles. "But we're not planning to waste any time getting you there, are we, sweetheart?"

Her face went even hotter. "The sooner the better," she returned sweetly.

Tyrus clapped Rourke on the back and then swept the blonde into his arms, pressing his hand against her abdomen. "Soon you'll have many babies like Martine and me."

Lisa was startled. Martine was Tyrus's wife?

"That's what we're hoping," Rourke drawled.

Lisa slid her hand out of Rourke's and reached for her bottled water. "How many children do you have?"

"Five," Tyrus said proudly.

Lisa barely kept her jaw from dropping. Martine didn't look old enough to have had five children. But then she didn't much look like a wife, given the way she'd planted that kiss on Rourke.

And judging by the amused glint in *his* eyes, he was probably reading her thoughts all too accurately.

She angled her chin and looked at the Harpers. "Rourke hasn't told me how you all met."

"Grif staked me when I first went into business for myself," Rourke answered. "I wouldn't be where I am now if not for him."

Griffin waved a hand. "An exaggeration. Rourke was always going places. Anyone who knew him could see that."

"Especially my niece," Nora added. Her gaze turned toward Lisa. "You could be her twin, you know."

Griffin laughed a little too heartily. "She's not interested in that, honey." He poured the last of the wine into their glasses and handed the bottle to Tyrus, who disappeared into the building again with Martine. "Is everything at the villa meeting your satisfaction?"

"As always," Rourke assured him.

Lisa could feel an awkward undercurrent, even if she couldn't interpret the cause. "The villa is yours?"

Nora nodded. "I've told Griffin that we should just sell it to Rourke. He's offered often enough. But my husband won't let it go." She smiled at him, wrinkling her nose. "Sentimental old fool that he is."

"We spent *our* honeymoon there," Griffin told Lisa. His hand was covering Nora's on top of the table.

It was very plain that they adored each other.

"He bought it a year later," Nora added. "Of course it needed a tremendous amount of renovations."

"Well, whatever changes you made, they were perfect. I've never seen such a beautiful place," Lisa said truthfully. "The terraces alone are—"

"Très romantique?" Martine had returned.

"Very…romantic," Lisa agreed. "But where do you stay if not your own villa?" She kept her focus on Nora, who seemed ever so much more pleasant than Martine and her voluptuous lips.

"We have an apartment here in the village. It's more convenient for us to be right here on a regular basis," Griffin told her. "We get back to New York only a few times a year, but that's where our main home is."

"My doctor is here in the village." Smiling, Nora rolled her eyes. "Grif is constantly shuttling me off to see him."

"Only because I want you with me as long as I can have you." Griffin cupped her cheek in his hand for a moment.

The moment felt intensely private to Lisa and she looked away, her gaze falling on Rourke.

His expression was hollow and, without thinking, she covered his clenched fist that rested on his thigh with her hand.

The feel of Lisa's hand on his drew Rourke's attention long enough for him to pull his dark thoughts out of the abyss where they'd fallen. She was watching him, her eyes soft. Concerned.

He loosened his tight fist and turned his palm until it met hers.

Her gaze flickered for a moment, but in the end stayed on his. A tentative smile fluttered around the corners of her soft lips and just that easily he was wishing strongly that they were back in the privacy of the villa.

He threaded his fingers through hers and she seemed content to stay that way until Tyrus brought lunch for all of them and she needed her hand to eat.

By the time they were finished, several hours had passed and the sun was even higher in the sky. Tyrus and Martine had been forced to leave the table in order to tend to the other customers who came to their bistro and Rourke could tell by the way Grif kept looking at Nora that it was time for them to be going as well, even though Nora kept dismissing the idea when Grif suggested it.

"As pleasant as this is," Rourke finally said with a deliberate grin, "this *is* our honeymoon. And I'm afraid my bride keeps me pretty bewitched." He rose from the table and went around to drop a kiss on Nora's softly lined cheek. "Take care of your old man, you hear?"

Nora laughed and patted his face. "That would be a switch,

wouldn't it?" She looked across the table at Lisa. "Taylor, dear, you and Rourke have got to visit us more often. Particularly when those babies finally start arriving. I want to be around to play with my grandnieces and nephews."

Rourke caught the way Lisa's smile wobbled a little and wished to hell that he'd thought ahead to this before hustling her into the village where he'd known it was likely they'd run into the Harpers.

"Nora, this is Lisa, not Taylor," Grif said patiently.

Nora's brows drew together, her confusion plain. "I… It is?" She looked at Lisa apologetically. "I'm so sorry, dear. You're a friend of Rourke's?"

"Yes," Lisa answered gently. "I'm a friend of Rourke's." She leaned over the table to clasp Nora's fluttering hands. "And I very much enjoyed meeting you and your husband."

The concern melted from Nora's face. "You are a dear." She looked up at Rourke. "I hope you realize she's a keeper."

Lisa's cheeks were pink as she straightened and sent him a fast glance. He slid his arm around her slender waist. "Don't worry, Nora. I know exactly what I've got."

He felt the way Lisa stiffened at that, but she didn't move away or say a word. Probably because she was too decent to cause Nora and Grif any concern.

Grif clasped Rourke's shoulder. "If we don't see you again before you head back to the States, we'll definitely see you in November at the awards gala in New York." His gaze switched to Lisa. "It's not every day that I get to present this guy with an award. I'm not going to let him miss it."

"It's on my calendar," Rourke assured him, wishing Grif would drop it.

But Lisa's interest was obviously already piqued. "What's the award for?"

"The G.R. Harper Philanthropic Award."

Lisa looked startled. "You're *that* Harper? There isn't anyone on the eastern seaboard who hasn't heard of that award."

Grif laughed. "My father instituted it. I'm just chairman of the family's foundation now. And thanks to guys like your husband who understand the importance of philanthropy, we're still in business helping thousands of people every year. But I'm preaching to the choir. You'd already know that."

Lisa smiled, no hint of the fact that she undoubtedly didn't, showing on her face. "Yes. Rourke is...quite something."

"And I wouldn't show at all if I could get out of it," Rourke reminded Grif.

"You'll show if only to shame other corporations into trying to win the award next year by giving even more money."

Since that was the truth of it, Rourke couldn't very well deny it. But at last, Grif dropped the subject and after a kiss on Lisa's cheek, he waved them off.

Lisa waited until they were out of sight of the bistro before she pulled away from him. "How much did you give?"

She would find out anyway when the awards deal rolled around, so he told her and her eyes widened. "Well. If you can give away that much, no wonder you can afford to fund the institute the way you are."

"Right. So can we drop it?"

"What makes you uncomfortable about it?"

He exhaled. "I'm not interested in getting accolades for just doing what's right."

She fell silent at that, but he could feel the speculative glances she kept throwing him. And she didn't speak again until they'd reached the car. "Does Nora have Alzheimer's?" Her voice was quiet.

At least she'd dropped the award. "They discovered it about a year ago." He pulled open her car door for her.

She sank into the seat and looked up at him. "I'm sorry."

"I believe you actually mean that." He could see it in her eyes that, in the sunlight, looked like translucent coffee.

Her lashes swept down suddenly, hiding those eyes altogether. She looked away and he thought briefly of his sister's claim that Lisa was shy. He'd dismissed it out of hand at the time, but maybe Tricia hadn't been so far off the mark, after all.

Lisa's fingers were smoothing the buttercup-yellow fabric of her dress over her legs. "Of course I mean it. It's perfectly clear that they're devoted to each other."

"They are." He rounded the car and slid behind the wheel and started the engine. "Not that they haven't had their trials, but they've always worked through them." He sighed deeply. "This one, though—" He felt his throat tighten and gunned the engine around a corner. "I don't know what Grif will do without her when that time comes."

"Rourke—" her voice softened "—that could still be a long way off, yet."

He nodded. Hoped.

"Her medical care here is good? I mean, this is a very small town. Wouldn't a larger facility have more treatment options?"

"The doctor she sees is an expert in the field. He focuses primarily on research and development. A lot like Ted's functions at the institute. The man's supposed to be a genius and this is where he wants to work. So…this is where they've stayed. And Nora is comfortable with him."

"Which is important to Griffin." She shielded her eyes from the sun with her hand as she watched him. "And they're both important to you."

"They've been good friends."

"Did you meet them because of Taylor?"

Given Nora's comments, he'd figured that question would come sooner or later whether he liked it or not. "No." It had been the other way around.

"So are you going to tell me who she is, or do I have to guess?"

He flexed his fingers around the steering wheel. "I imagine you've figured it out."

"She's your ex-wife." Her tone had cooled again. Sympathy no longer evident. "Whom I evidently resemble. A lot."

"My very *ex*-wife who bears a passing resemblance," he said abruptly. "You interested in seeing Nice? It wouldn't take long to drive there."

"And yet you *claim* you were never at the villa with her." She ignored his attempted side trip—both verbal and literal. "Seems unlikely when the place belongs to her aunt and uncle."

"I was never at the villa with Taylor," he repeated evenly. "Not before we married, not during our marriage and sure in hell not after it was over."

"Why not?"

"What difference does it make? Just because I like the place doesn't mean she did."

"Who wouldn't like it?"

She sounded indignant, and he almost wanted to laugh. "Let's just say that the villa was a little too laid-back for her tastes." Those had run more toward glitter and excitement versus peaceful tranquility. And he really didn't want to talk—or think—about his ex-wife any more than necessary.

"So how *did* you meet the Harpers?"

He slanted a look toward her. "You're very full of questions this afternoon. Why?"

That slender hand shading her eyes also shaded the expression in them. "We're married. People will expect us to know these sorts of things about each other." She hesitated for a moment. "If we're going to be…having a child together…we should at least have honesty between us. Know these sorts of things about each other."

"There's no *if* about it." Not anymore. Not thanks to the combined brilliance of Bonner and Demetrious.

"Fine. *Since* there will be a child, we should know this kind of stuff. Or at least make some attempt at knowing each other better if we want to make this work at all." Her chin lifted. "Or do you disagree?"

He didn't disagree. On the other hand, he was pretty curious why she was suddenly seeming as agreeable as she was. "Grif was a visiting professor in one of my sophomore university classes. Oddly enough, we hit it off."

"Why odd?"

He slowed to a stop at a crossroads. "Because I was cheating on an exam. Now, do you want to go into the city or not?"

"Why were you cheating?"

"Because it was easier than studying and I hated English lit. He should have kicked me out of the class."

"But he didn't."

"No. He didn't. And in the end, pretty much everything I know about being a decent man, I learned from him." He exhaled. "Grif wouldn't exactly approve of our arrangement."

"You knew what being good meant before you went to college. You told me you were a Boy Scout, remember?"

"A rotten one," he drawled.

"What happened to your father?"

"Enough questions for now. Nice or not?"

She looked one way down the empty road. Then the other. "Not."

He turned the car in the direction of the villa.

"Tyrus and Martine seem very friendly. Particularly Martine."

He hid a smile. Yeah, Martine had really bugged her. Not that it was unusual. Martine had a way of bugging most women. "They're interesting people. Tyrus used to own a five-star hotel in Paris."

"And his wife?" The last word had a decided edge to it.

"Adores him."

She huffed softly. "Really. She goes around kissing *every-one* like that? Or does she just reserve that particular greeting for you?"

"Admit it." He ran his finger down the nape of her neck. "You *are* jealous. First it was Sylvie. Now it's Martine?"

"Please. I just feel sorry for Tyrus."

"Tyrus is as proud of his attractive wife as he is proud of his hellion kids."

"And he doesn't mind that you and his wife are—" She gave him an eyebrow-arched look.

"Are nothing."

"Then what were you kissing her for?"

"Maybe you need glasses, princess. Martine was kissing me."

"You didn't exactly beat her off with a stick!"

"And offend Tyrus?"

She made a disgusted sound.

He laughed softly. "Martine kisses every man she knows. Tyrus doesn't mind because he knows he's the one she goes home with at night. And cheating for me extended only as far as English lit tests and that was a lifetime ago. I don't cheat on my women, nor do I share them."

"Is that supposed to be a warning or something?"

His humor dried up as rapidly as a desert rain. "Take it how you see fit. Once the terms of our marriage are met, you can do what you want." He was reminding himself as much as her.

"And if there's another man I want?"

"If there was another man you wanted now, we wouldn't even be here."

"You don't know that. You're the one with the money to save the institute."

"If you were truly involved with someone, you would have found another way than me."

"I think there may actually be a compliment in there."

He shrugged.

"Maybe there will be a man later on."

When a woman looked like Lisa there was always going to be plenty of men vying for that position. The thought was dark. "Don't expect me to come chasing after you."

"Why would you?" She dashed a lock of hair away from her cheek where it had blown loose from that infernal knot of hers. "It's not like you're in love with me."

"Wouldn't matter even if I were. If a woman betrays me, she can keep walking right out the door."

She slid him a long look. "Is that what Taylor did? Cheat on you?"

Bits of gravel spun beneath the tires when he turned up the drive to the villa. He thought about not answering. Thought, too, about the logic in her assessment that there were some things they'd naturally be expected to know about each other. The reason behind the demise of his first marriage was probably one of those things. "Yes."

"I'm sorry."

He grimaced. "She wasn't."

"Would it have mattered if she were? How long were you married?"

"Four years. Not long enough for me to even consider forgiving that." The cheating wasn't the worst, anyway, though he had no intentions of getting into that. It was who Taylor had chosen to cheat *with*. And why. "And before you ask again, it was over nearly five years ago."

"Then you were married pretty young."

Out of college and on the way to his second million. "Doesn't excuse it."

She made a soft *hmm.* "I don't see how couples ever get over a betrayal like that, no matter how long they've been together," she added after a moment.

"Some recover from it. If they want to badly enough." He'd seen that in action. But then he didn't possess the same kind of fiber that made up a man like Griffin Harper.

And he'd never loved anyone the way that Grif loved Nora. Not even Taylor.

Lisa was shaking her head. "Not me. Lies are unforgiveable enough, but that strikes me as the very worst kind."

"Then we're more alike than either one of us thought."

She watched him for a long while. "That ought to be a frightening thought," she finally said.

"That there might be something we actually have in common?"

"Yes."

"But you're not frightened."

She sucked in her lower lip for a moment, leaving it distractingly moist. "No."

Then she sat back in her seat, leaving him with the disturbing knowledge that things would have been safer between them if she were.

Chapter Nine

When they arrived at the villa, there was no sign of Marta or Sylvie and, contrarily, Lisa found herself wishing that there had been.

Because now, the silence only underscored her and Rourke's privacy.

Honeymoon privacy.

Maybe she should have told Rourke she wanted to go to Nice, after all.

Aware of his gaze on her like some physical thing, she crossed the living area to the doors and pushed them open, letting in the balmy, vaguely sweet-scented air. She toed off her espadrilles and walked out onto the terrace, and folded her arms over the top of the stone balustrade.

Below, the ocean glittered sapphire blue. Beyond the narrow line of beach, the hillside rose sharply, verdant with fat trees and tall palms.

"How could anyone *not* love this?" she wondered aloud. "It's so perfectly beautiful."

Rourke joined her at the rail. "Yes. It is."

But a glance at him told her he wasn't looking at the view, but at her.

There was no way to will away the flush that began climbing her cheeks. She turned her gaze resolutely back out to the sea. "Do you sail?" There were several boats out in the water.

"Occasionally. Are you shy?"

Her cheeks warmed even more. She tried a laugh, but it only came off sounding nervous. "What makes you ask that?"

"Tricia mentioned it. I told her she was off base."

"Well, there you go, then." What was the point of telling him that his sister was closer to the mark than he was?

His forearm was pressing alongside hers on top of the warm stone and it took every ounce of willpower she possessed not to move her tingling arm away from his. "When I was young, we went sailing as often as we could."

"Your family?"

She suddenly wished she hadn't even brought it up. That was what she got for trying to focus on something other than Rourke's overwhelmingly masculine appeal. "Derek," she admitted slowly. "Dad took me one time. It was Memorial Day weekend. Usually he was too busy to ever go, and my mother—" She shook her head. "Sailing wasn't exactly her cup of tea." Her lips twisted a little. "Would have mussed her hair."

"Like this?" Rourke tucked the strands of hair that had fallen loose from her chignon during the drive behind her ear.

She swallowed hard, unable to find her voice just then.

Rourke's hand went back to the railing. His forearm back to scorching hers. "What about Paul and Olivia?"

Her throat eased a little. "Paul had his own interests—usually his studies—and Olivia was always dancing." She didn't want to think about how much time Derek had always been willing to give her when she'd been growing up.

He'd been her pal, taking her sailing or to hockey games.

Her confidant, listening without judgment when she'd railed against Emily's stringent standards about the behavior of proper young ladies or when she'd been left alone on the night of every school dance because nobody had asked her out.

He'd even been her hero, helping her to see the value she had where the institute was concerned.

And now, she wanted to hate him for the position he'd put them all in. She did hate him. But she couldn't help still loving him.

"I can't believe what he did," she admitted. "Can't understand why."

The silence ticked between them, broken only by the hushed rustle of the palm fronds extending over the terrace. "He checked into a rehab center, if that helps you with the why."

Shocked, she looked up at Rourke. He was standing even more closely than she'd thought. "Rehab for what? When? And how do *you* know?"

"For what, I don't know. But it was Saturday. And that I know because my media director kept a story about it from seeing the light of day. I told you that I would do what I can to keep the institute and your brother's actions out of the press."

She remembered the bits of Rourke's phone conversation that she'd overheard the day they'd arrived. "I wasn't sure you'd meant it."

"I gave you my word."

This close, she could have counted every one of his thick, spiky eyelashes. "I've always thought you were impossibly arrogant." Her voice was little more than a whisper. "But I think there might actually be a wide streak of decency in there."

"And I used to think you were just an ice princess. Turns

out that's just a mask you wear to keep anyone from seeing the heat that's inside. Same as this knot you wear hides those long, wild waves." He reached behind her head and she felt him pluck one of the pins out of her hair.

It dropped to the smooth stone beneath their feet with a soft ping. Soon, it was followed by another. And another.

Her mouth went dry. Her heart felt as if it was climbing up into her throat. "Do I remind you of your ex-wife? Is that what the attraction is?" She feared knowing the answer because she wasn't sure if it would even matter. Not with the way he made her heart pound.

"If you really reminded me of her, there would be no attraction," he said so flatly that she couldn't help believe him.

He pulled every pin from her hair, unwinding it and threading his fingers through it until it hung over her shoulders and down her back. When he seemed satisfied, his hands drifted to the buttons that lined the front of her snug bodice. His knuckles brushed against her as he deliberately undid the top one.

She exhaled shakily.

His head lowered. He slowly kissed the point of her shoulder, almost distracting her from the release of a second button. And a third. "Are you going to protest?" His words whispered against her neck, below her ear, more seduction than question.

Did she even want to? Hadn't she known this would happen when she'd declined driving to Nice?

"No." The word was barely audible.

"Good." Between them, she felt the bodice of her dress loosening. Inching downward.

A bird flew overhead, cawing loudly. She could barely hear the sound of the ocean above the pounding of her heart.

Then he slid one hand behind her head, catching the nape of her neck, his gaze locked on hers as he slowly pressed his mouth against hers and the only thing she knew then was the darkly seductive taste of him. The only thing she cared about was the feel of his hands on her.

He was devouring her by slow degrees and she didn't care.

He tore his mouth from hers, lips burning against her jaw, his breath as ragged as hers. He lifted his head, staring down at her as he took a step back. His hands were on her shoulders, fingers burning hotter than the sunshine.

Her loosened bodice fell away, the folds of her dress caught only by the swell of her hips. The sweet, warm air drifted over her bare breasts, her achingly tight nipples.

He twined his fingers gently in her hair, tugging her head back until she looked up at him.

"This is who I see when I look at you." His voice was low. Husky. "Fire in your eyes. Lips naked and soft. Skin warm and waiting."

"Then you're the only one," she admitted, feeling oddly thrilled. Wholly aroused.

"I could spend an hour or two explaining how wrong you are." His hands slid down her bare spine, pushing the dress beyond her hips, and the cotton crumpled around her ankles. Her feet. "But I've got better things in mind." He caught her hips and lifted her right off her feet and out of the dress.

She gasped and caught his shoulders more tightly.

"Put your legs around me."

Trembling wildly, she did, and he turned away from the balustrade to walk across the terrace. She pressed her head against his shoulder, agonizingly aware of the hard press of his chest beneath the soft friction of his linen shirt. He carried her down the steps to the lower terrace and nudged through the French doors of the bedroom.

It was cooler inside. And dimmer, thanks to the slant of the shutters on the windows. He left the door open and carried her to the wide bed, settling her in the center.

Her hands slowly fell away. She stared up at him as he began flicking open the buttons on his shirt. "I thought you were heading down to the beach." Her gaze felt glued to the expanding wedge of muscular chest he was revealing.

"Disappointed?" He reached the last button and tossed the shirt aside. His narrow belt jangled softly as he pulled it loose.

She swallowed. Hard. "Maybe," she admitted faintly.

His lips curved. His pants stayed where they fell, and so did the body-hugging boxers beneath. He bent one knee on the mattress, slowly moving toward her.

She knew she was staring, but there didn't seem to be anything she could do about it. Everything about him was hard. The muscles roping his shoulders. The ridges of his abdomen.

"We'll make love on the beach," he murmured, settling between her thighs where she felt that hardest part press insistently between them. "And anywhere else we want." His hands burned over her thighs, guiding them along his hips. "As often as we want."

Her fingers pressed into his chest. The swirl of dark hair there felt softly crisp against her palms. "You'll change your mind." The words came without warning, probably pushed out by the sudden tightness in her chest.

"I seriously doubt it." He turned onto his back, pulling her with him until she was draped over him like a wet blanket. "I've wanted you for months." His hands caught her face. Drew her closer. "Turn off that brain for a while, Lisa."

Her chest felt even tighter. "But I'm not any good at this," she warned miserably.

He didn't move a muscle. Didn't even seem to breathe for a moment. "I'm going to assume that some fool told you that. Because I know you're too smart to come up with such an asinine idea." His voice seemed to rumble up from deep within his chest, vibrating against her.

She straightened her arms, finding some distance between her racing heart and his. "But it's true. I'm not good with…with men."

He eyed her for a moment and even though she was shaking with desire, she still felt like a bug on the head of a pin.

And knew that she was the one who'd stuck herself there.

He pushed up on his arm suddenly, and without letting her go, pulled her with him up the mattress until his back was against the carved headboard. "No men," he said quietly. "Just one man." His hands slid slowly down her back, then slid up again. "Me." None of the fire had left his eyes but there was a watchfulness there that made her throat tight. "Are you afraid I'm going to hurt you?"

"No." Not in the sense that he meant.

"Are you a virgin?"

She shook her head yet again, this time flushing. "Of course not."

"When were you last with a man? Six months? A year? Two?"

"Seven." She was grateful that he didn't gape at her. "He was a guy in college."

"The only guy?"

She groaned and covered her face with her hand. "I should wear a muzzle," she muttered. "Then maybe my stupid tongue would stop getting in the way."

His chest lifted and fell with the choked laugh he gave. "I have plenty of thoughts about your tongue. None of them involves a muzzle, believe me." He pulled her hands away from her face. "There's nobody here in this bed but you and me. You have just as much control as I do." His lips twisted slightly. "More, when it comes down to it, because as much as I want you—and it's gotta be obvious as hell to you that I do—you're still the one who can say no."

Which she'd been doing all along. And which he'd actually been respecting, she realized, no matter what the terms of their agreement were.

"Will you trust me?" He tipped her chin up. "At least in this?"

"I want to," she admitted helplessly, surprising even herself by the truth of it.

"Good enough," he said softly. He slowly rubbed his thumb over her lower lip. "Kiss me."

She blinked. Moistened her lip only to taste the faint saltiness of the tip of his thumb. Her gaze flicked to his and she caught the flex of a muscle in his hard jaw.

Still he waited for her to make the move.

She leaned closer and brushed her lips across his. Felt the surprising softness, the unexpectedly lush curve of his lower lip. A faint sound rose in her throat and she sank a little deeper against his chest. Her hand roved over one wide, muscled shoulder; slid against the strong column of his brown neck and felt the push of his pulse against her fingertips.

That tattooing beat seemed as deeply intimate as the feel of his body pushing against her increasingly damp panties.

She grazed the tip of her tongue over his lip. Caught it lightly between her teeth.

His hands suddenly closed tightly around her hips only to ease off a second later.

What fascinated her more? That unexpected, uncontrolled motion? Or the very deliberate control he exercised over it?

She tilted her head slightly. Settled her mouth over his, tentatively tasting the inner curve of his lip, feeling the ridge of sharp teeth.

One of his hands shifted, slid over her rear, hovered over the elastic edge of her panties.

Her tongue found his and his chest expanded against her breasts. Like a needy cat, she felt herself arching against him, wanting more of that. Wanting more of his hands on the curve of her bottom, wanting more of the press of him between her legs.

She pulled her mouth from his, hauling in a shuddering breath.

"Tell me what you feel." His low voice was even huskier. More ragged.

"You," she breathed.

His teeth flashed. His fingers flexed against her spine. "Too obvious. *How* you feel."

He was in her head more than he was in her body. As little as a day—maybe even a matter of hours—earlier, and she would have shied away from that. From him.

She ran her hands down his arms, circled the sinewy wrists, then caught his hands. She drew them between them. Slowly pushed them flat and pressed her mouth to one palm, then the other.

Then she pressed his palms to her breasts.

"I feel empty," she whispered. "And I want you to fill me."

His hands cupped her breasts, shaped them. Thumbs roved over her drawn nipples, sending waves of need to the clutching space inside her. When his hands left her, she wanted to protest, but that desire died instead in the moist fire of his mouth closing over her while he shifted and bore her steadily down onto the mattress.

And then his tongue was branding a line down her abdomen, the edge of her underwear, and then beneath as he dragged the bit of cotton down her thighs and right off her legs.

Her hands frantically caught at his shoulders. "Rourke—"

He stopped. Looked at her. A dark angel in devil's disguise. "Yes?" The word whispered intimately against her.

She could barely breathe. "Yes," she sighed, and nearly bowed off the bed with splintering pleasure when his mouth settled on her.

She was still quaking long moments later when just as deliberately, he kissed his way back up her belly. Over her breasts. Pressing his palms flat against hers, he slowly, inexorably pressed into her.

Filled her.

And even though she'd wanted this—wanted him—she hadn't expected to feel as if he were filling every cell that formed her, every thought that made her. She couldn't tell where she ended and he began. Couldn't tell if it was her body tightening all over again or his thickening even more with indescribable pleasure. Didn't know if it was the beat of her heart thundering against her breast, or if it was his. Didn't care that his name was a crying chant on her lips and loved it that her name was like a prayer on his.

Filling wasn't the right word at all, she realized faintly when everything they were coalesced into one…glorious… perfect…climax.

Joining was.

"So tell me about the idiot from your college days."

Her world had finally stopped spinning, righted once more even if a part of her wondered if it could ever really be the same. She'd regained the ability to breathe, as well, but Rourke's head resting against her breast was still a distraction.

She lifted his hand from her belly and toyed with his fingers, watching the play of light that slanted through the French doors catch in the platinum of their wedding rings. "I've forgotten all about him."

He laughed softly.

She found herself smiling, too. "He was in my economics class. His name was Skyler and I thought I was in love with him. He claimed he loved me, too, but after we slept together—mistake that it was—he dumped me. Said he needed a woman in his bed, not a stick who didn't know how to enjoy herself."

"What'd you do?"

"Besides believe him?" She shook her head. "I made such good grades that on the grading curve he ended up failing the class."

Rourke pushed up on his elbow. His hair was falling rakishly over his forehead. "Good girl." He kissed her arm. "And no man worth his salt should blame a woman for her lack of pleasure."

"Did you learn that bit of wisdom from Griffin, too?"

He shook his head, his grin quick and deeply wicked. "That came from a very smart cookie named Janelle who kindly introduced me to the ways of women."

She rolled her eyes. "And how old were you when this angel of mercy descended upon you?"

"Good choice of words," he drawled. "Sixteen. She was a much advanced twenty with an amazing arsenal of knowledge at her disposal."

She let out a huff and rolled onto her stomach. "Your mother would have been appalled."

"My mother never knew." He gave her a playful slap on the rump. "Get your lazy rear up. I'm starving."

She wanted nothing more than to sleep. "Typical."

"I *am* a man."

She couldn't help her smile, even if it did look goofy. "I noticed." She rescued one of the pillows from the foot of the bed where it had somehow ended up and tucked it beneath her cheek with a satisfied sigh. "You won't have to hunt or forage far, I'm sure. Not with Marta and Sylvie at your beck and call."

"Not quite. I told them we wouldn't need them after all while we're here."

Surprised, she opened her eyes and looked at him. "Since when?"

"Since you were in the shower this morning." With her hair streaming around her and her eyes looking slumberous and satisfied, it was all Rourke could do not to roll Lisa onto her back and make love to her all over again. Instead, he leaned over and satisfied himself by kissing the freckle on her neck and then the small of her back before sliding off the bed and moving away from temptation. "They made you feel self-conscious. So they had to go."

Not bothering with finding some clothes, he headed out of the room, carrying her bemused expression with him.

"You did pay attention when I said I couldn't cook," her voice called after him, "didn't you?"

He stopped and stuck his head back in the doorway. "You also claimed you were no good in the sack," he drawled. "Didn't believe you then. Don't believe you now." He yanked his head back from the doorway just in time to miss the pillow that she threw at him.

But he could hear her laughter as he headed away from the bedroom, and was smiling himself as he went.

While he might have sent Marta away, she'd still managed to leave an assortment of food in the fridge and he pulled out an apple and a bottle of water before going into the office, where he found a half-dozen messages on his cell phone. He returned only one, though, to Ted Bonner.

"Find the cure to cancer yet?" he asked when Ted picked up.

His friend's laugh sounded as if it were next door and not halfway around the world. "That's not the cure you used to be interested in."

Rourke supposed it was proof of how far he'd come since the day he'd learned that his and Taylor's failure to conceive a child hadn't been because of her infertility, but *his* that he could now laugh about it. "Believe me, buddy, I'm still interested. And grateful to be the first subject in your trial. First kid we have is gonna be named after you and Chance."

"Pity the kid if she's a girl, then. You're taking the compound?"

"As prescribed. And the vitamins. And eating right. Drinking plenty of water." He toasted his friend with the bottled water even though Ted couldn't see it. "Following all the protocols you've given me."

"We're going to have to expand the study, you know," Ted reminded him for about the millionth time.

"Say the word when you're ready," Rourke said, also for about the millionth time. "You know where your funding is coming from." And when a noninvasive, natural supplement hit the market to improve one of the causes of male infertility, they'd all be singing lullabies all the way to the bank. Nothing of which he and Ted and Chance hadn't already discussed at length. "So what'd you really call about, anyway?"

"Just wanted to share the good news. Sara Beth's pregnant."

"No kidding. Congratulations, man!" Genuine pleasure filled his voice.

"Yeah. I'm still wondering how it happened." Ted laughed. "Well, you know what I mean. Don't tell your wife yet, though. Sara Beth wants to tell Lisa herself."

"No prob."

"Who knows," Ted went on. "If you and Lisa end up with that honeymoon baby you say you're hoping for, our kids could be in Scouts together someday."

"Yeah." Rourke slowly set the bottle down on the desk. A short while later, Ted hung up and Rourke left the office and the rest of his voice messages unreturned.

He walked back to the bedroom. Lisa wasn't lying in bed anymore, but he could hear the sound of the shower and he followed it into the bathroom, where he could clearly see her through the glass block of the shower wall.

He went over to the opening and looked at her lithe body, silky suds slowly sliding down her limbs while steam shrouded around her.

Her gaze warmed as she looked back at him.

"Want company?"

Her lashes dipped shyly, but only for a moment. Then she looked back at him and nodded.

And when he stepped into the steam with her, he knew he wasn't thinking about making a honeymoon baby any more than he'd been thinking about it earlier.

The only thing he was thinking about was Lisa.

And that most definitely hadn't been part of the deal.

Chapter Ten

"Ohmigosh. Look how tanned you are." Sara Beth stopped in the doorway of Lisa's office at the institute and propped her hands on her hips. "Obviously honeymooning in the south of France for the better part of a month agrees with you."

At the sight of her friend, Lisa jumped from behind her desk where she'd been studying health insurance bids and went over to hug her. "Not as much as marriage seems to be agreeing with you," she countered, laughing. She stepped back to look over Sara Beth. "You're positively glowing."

Sara Beth's cheeks were almost as pink as the scrubs she was wearing. "Marriage is pretty good," she said, clearly understating. She stepped into the office and closed the door. "So tell me how the trip was. *Ooh la la* romantic? Hot monkey sex every time you turned around?"

Lisa headed back to her desk, ducking her head a little. "It was…pretty good," she returned.

Sara Beth let out a laughing groan. "Now that's just not fair." She leaned her hip on the corner of Lisa's desk. "At least—" she lifted her eyebrows "—tell me you didn't earn that tan sitting on the beach while you were poring over files from this place."

"I had fun," Lisa admitted slowly. Which wasn't at all what she'd expected.

Sara Beth lifted the glossy business magazine that was sitting opened on the edge of Lisa's desk, featuring a black and white shot of Rourke helping Lisa out of the limousine on the day of their wedding. *The Ties that Bind...or Blind?* was the article's headline. "Not every analyst thinks investing in the institute is the best business bet for Rourke. They are saying he did it for you."

"And Rourke's answer to that is in the article. The reporter tracked us down in France last week." After that momentous day when Rourke had turned her world upside down, the reporter's visit had been the sole intrusion of the life waiting for their return.

The rest of the time, she and Rourke had done exactly what most honeymooning couples did. They'd explored the countryside and strolled in marketplaces. They'd had lunch with the Harpers more than once, and even Martine had stopped greeting Rourke with that plastering kiss. They'd lazed on the beach and they'd even slept under the stars on the terrace outside their bedroom.

And they'd made love.

Again. And again. And again.

And if it weren't for the fact that Lisa had known that idyllic time would have to end when he returned to New York and she to Boston, it would have been painfully easy to forget the reason they were there at all.

Sara Beth held up the magazine and read. "'Indulging my

bride is my greatest pleasure, reports the newly wedded Devlin,'" she quoted. "'But nothing gets in the way of business. And the future of the Armstrong Fertility Institute is good business.'" She looked up. "Sounds great for the institute. What does the blushing bride think?"

Lisa lifted her shoulder. "Business *is* business. Just because we put these—" she lifted her hand, waggling her wedding rings "—on our fingers doesn't mean that's changed." He'd put her on the plane back to Boston where she'd get back to business and he'd stayed in New York where he'd get back to *his*.

They'd get together on weekends.

Sara Beth's expression had gone serious. "Then you *did* marry him for the money." She hopped off the desk before Lisa could form a reply. "I was afraid something was off even before the I do's. But everything happened in such a rush it was easy to buy into the whole sweeping-you-off-your-feet scenario. Tell me I'm wrong."

"It's not like that," Lisa protested. Not exactly. Not anymore. Not since she'd found the man beneath the money and he'd found the woman beneath the suit.

Sara Beth propped her hands on her hips, staring her down. "Are you in love with him?"

Lisa blinked, for some reason caught off guard. "Not every marriage is about love," she hedged. "There's mutual respect and common interests and—"

"Sex?"

Her cheeks suddenly blazed and Sara Beth, being Sara Beth, didn't fail to notice. "You *are* sleeping with him!"

"Good grief," Lisa muttered, shaking her head. "Thank heavens you shut the door. Yes, I'm sleeping with him. He's my husband. He wants a child and he doesn't want to wait."

Sara Beth's long ponytail slid over her shoulder as she

cocked her head, pinning Lisa with a studying stare. "What do you want?"

Keeping secrets from Sara Beth was nearly impossible. "I want what he wants," she said, which was close enough to the truth, wasn't it?

Sara Beth's eyes narrowed, but thankfully she didn't challenge that. "So, was he worth the wait after Skyler-the-Dweeb?"

Lisa's mouth opened. Closed. She blinked. "Definitely."

Sara Beth let out her breath in a whoosh and collapsed into one of the chairs in front of Lisa's desk. "Well, at least there's hope, then."

Lisa jostled the pile of bids into a neat stack. "Hope for what?"

"Your happily ever after."

She couldn't help herself. She laughed. "You are *such* a romantic."

"Yup." Sara Beth leaned back in the chair, her hands clasped over her tummy. "A pregnant romantic, as it happens."

Now it was Lisa's turn to stare. "What?"

"Dr. and Mrs. Bonner are pleased to announce the future arrival of baby Bonner." Sara Beth's smile positively dripped happiness. "It's soon, of course. And we weren't exactly trying, but then again, we weren't exactly *not* trying, if you know what I mean. And this isn't just another pregnancy scare," Sara Beth added, obviously no longer troubled by the time she'd feared she was pregnant, before Ted had proposed. "All tests positive and systems are a go." She grinned.

Sara Beth and Ted had been married barely half a year. They hadn't even been intentionally trying.

Beneath the cover of the desk, Lisa pressed her hand against her abdomen. There was no question that Rourke *was* trying to make a baby.

Yes, he was making certain that the process was mind-blowing, but she couldn't afford to let herself forget the underlying purpose.

For all she knew, she'd already conceived. She would probably know later that week, if her period arrived as usual.

And if she were pregnant, what would become of hers and Rourke's relationship? His real interest in her was her uterus, after all. And while she'd claimed to be just as anxious to get that accomplished as he was—because it meant getting closer to the end of their arrangement—a claim was all it was.

Pregnancy in theory was one thing.

Pregnancy in reality meant a child. Becoming a mother.

"Helloooo. Earth to Lisa."

She realized that Sara Beth had been talking to her and felt herself flush all over again. "Sorry?"

Sara Beth's eyes danced. "Reliving a little French bliss?"

Lisa ignored that. "So how are you feeling? You're going to be a great mother. And I—" she smiled, truly happy for her friend "—am going to make a great honorary auntie."

Sara Beth's smile trembled a little. "Yes, you are." She cleared her throat. "And aside from an occasional desire to throw up on a patient's shoes, I'm feeling marvelous. We haven't told anyone around here, yet. I wanted you to be the first to know."

"Okay, you've gotta stop or we're going to be blubbering idiots, here." Lisa snatched a tissue from the box on her credenza and swiped her nose.

"What about you and Rourke? Any possibility of a honeymoon baby?"

Lisa managed a nod and Sara Beth's eyes sparkled. "We could be pregnant together." She looked thrilled by the very idea of it.

"Rourke's coming to town Friday night for the weekend," Lisa offered, wanting to get off the subject of her becoming pregnant. "We should all get together then and celebrate your and Ted's good news."

"Perfect. You know, you sounded very married, just then." Sara Beth picked up the small clock sitting on the corner of Lisa's desk, then put it back and pushed to her feet. "That's the deal, then? You're in your separate cities during the workweek and together on the weekends?"

"We decided that before the wedding. I told you."

"Yeah, but…" Sara Beth wrinkled her nose. "I would sure miss Ted if we were apart every week like that. Although—" she lifted a finger "—all those special homecomings could have an appeal, too. Candlelight dinner. Sexy lingerie…" She grinned mischievously. "Of course, unless you've taken up shopping since you've been hobnobbing with the wealthy Côte d'Azur folks, I know for a fact that your drawers aren't exactly filled with those sorts of *drawers*."

Lisa deliberately made a face. "Don't you have a patient waiting?"

Sara Beth laughed and, with a wave, headed out of the office. "I'm done for the day just before lunch. Call me. We'll go shopping at my favorite lingerie store. You can get something totally out of character for you, and I can get something sexy to wear before I can't fit in it anymore!" Her rubber-soled shoes squeaked a little as she hurried down the corridor.

Lisa looked down at the papers on her desk, but her gaze fell on the magazine. She'd bought it at the newsstand on her way into work that morning and could have recited the article from memory by now.

Business is business. Rourke's words to the reporter might as well have been underlined and highlighted in neon for the way they seemed to jump out at her.

She'd been on the terrace, sitting at the table with the reporter and Rourke when he'd given the interview. She knew exactly what he'd said. The expressions on his face when he'd said them. And nothing in the article was a misrepresentation.

And she hadn't lied to Sara Beth. Business *was* business.

So why did Rourke's comment nag at her?

Annoyed with herself, she flipped the magazine closed and stuffed it into the bottom drawer of her desk. Her phone buzzed and she snatched it up. "Yes?"

"Had a lot of work piled up on your desk waiting for you?"

Something inside her chest seemed to squeeze at the unexpected sound of Rourke's voice. "Hi. And no, the pile hasn't been too bad." She glossed over the stacks of correspondence and reports and messages that she'd been wading through for two solid hours. "What's, um, what's wrong?"

His laugh was low and rasped over her nerve endings in a wholly disruptive way. "There has to be something wrong for me to call my wife?" His voice dropped another notch. "I *really* missed you this morning. Waking up without you in my arms was no fun at all."

Her mouth went more than a little dry. She glanced at the opened doorway of her office. Thankfully, her assistant, Ella, was busy with a telephone call at the desk she occupied outside Lisa's office. "I had to come back to work," she reminded him.

"I know." His voice suddenly sounded even nearer. "But one of the advantages of being the boss is that I can tell my business to follow—" he suddenly appeared in her doorway "—where I want it to go." He grinned faintly, snapping his cell phone shut.

She shot up from her chair so fast, it rolled back and banged the credenza behind her desk. "Rourke!"

"Is that a happy-to-see-me 'Rourke'?"

Her stomach jumped around giddily. "I didn't expect to see you until Friday night."

His lips tilted, amused. "I'll take that as a yes, because it suits me." He seemed to roll his shoulder around the door frame as he entered, and very deliberately closed the door behind him. "You look very…icy."

His eyes were anything but as he slowly advanced, and she moistened her lips, dashing her hands down the front of her pale gray suit. "Would you prefer I come to work in a red leather miniskirt?"

"Nobody'd get any work done if they saw the rest of the legs you're hiding under these skinny skirts of yours." He hooked his arm around her waist and pulled her to him.

She supposed she should be a little offended at his macho tactic, but her heart was too busy jiggling around in her throat to worry too deeply. "What are you doing here?"

His fingers kneaded her hips through the fine wool suit. "Checking on my investment?"

She couldn't help the bubble of laughter that rose to her lips. "You're terrible."

His lips tilted. "That's not what you were saying last night," he reminded her, dropping a much-too-brief kiss on her lips. "Then it was more on the order of 'you're good, you're perfect, right there, oh, yes—'"

She clamped her hand over his mouth. "All right. Enough. This is a place of business."

"Where babies are made." He pressed a kiss to the palm of her hand before pulling it away and tugging her even closer until their hips met. "Coincidentally enough."

She sucked in a breath, nearly swaying. "How do you do it?" Her voice was breathless. "Make me want you like this?" They'd made love less than twelve hours ago. They'd returned from France in the afternoon, had dinner with his mother in the city, and before Rourke had driven Lisa to the private airfield where his jet was waiting to fly her back to Boston, had driven her mad in the foyer of his penthouse apartment.

They hadn't even made it as far as the bedroom.

"Lucky, I guess." His hands worked the buttons on her suit jacket, and delved inside to discover the camisole that was all she wore beneath it. Her nipple rose tight and eager through the thin, plain cotton and she had a fleeting thought of Sara Beth's lingerie shopping idea. "If we didn't need to meet with your management team in five minutes, I'd be asking if that office door has a lock on it."

"Management team." The reminder was almost as effective as a bucket of ice water. She met every week with her department heads. That day was even more important, since she was coming off a long absence, and they had to begin dealing with Rourke's influx of cash.

She hastily backed away from him, hurriedly redoing the buttons, a task that would have been much easier if her fingers weren't shaking and her body weren't yearning for his. "Is that what you really came for?"

"It's one of the reasons." He sat on the edge of her desk, watching her fuss with her jacket. "Not the only one."

She supposed she should be grateful for that.

She reached the top button of the jewel-neck collar and flipped the narrow silver necklace she wore out over it before picking up the leather-bound pad that held her agenda and meeting notes. "You didn't mention it before."

"You didn't mention the management meeting," he pointed out. "I learned that from Ella."

She stopped in front of him, holding her pad against her breasts like a schoolgirl. "Is this what it will be like? You going around me to find out about the operational matters of the institute? Pulling rank on me?"

"Don't get your panties in a knot," he drawled, looking amused. "Ella sent me your schedule first thing this morning the same way she'd been sending me your schedule before the wedding."

The explanation was perfectly logical but it still put her on edge. She was way over her head when it came to him on a personal basis. She wasn't certain at all how she felt about him being underfoot here at the institute. This was her turf. Her comfort zone.

"Stop looking worried," he chided as he straightened. "I've told you that I had no problem with the way this place was being run to begin with. Except for the blind faith you all put in your CFO," he added pointedly. "All I want to do is observe and meet all the players." He held out one arm. "After you."

She gave him a narrow look, but aware of the time ticking and loathe to be late for anything, she stepped past him and headed out of the office.

The boardroom where they usually met was on the top floor of their building. When they arrived, Paul and Ted were already sitting at the enormous oval table dominating the center of the sunlit room. Ted got up, greeting Rourke with a wide smile and a clap on the shoulder and, leaving them to it, she assumed her usual spot at the table, glancing at the clock on the wall as the room quickly filled. At five minutes past, her gaze scanned those present. "Where's Dr. Demetrios?"

"Here." The handsome, swarthy doctor entered, his white lab coat trailing out behind him. "Got a mom-in-the-making getting prepped." His brown eyes sparkled with good humor. "So I'll give you about five minutes."

Lisa wasn't surprised. She well knew the doctor preferred to be bedside than boardroom table-side. "All right, then you and Dr. Bonner can report out first." She opened her pad and picked up her pen, taking an occasional note while Ted and Chance both launched into concise updates of their current work.

"We may be looking at an expanded study very soon," Ted concluded. "A natural supplement that increases sperm motility. Our early testing is looking really promising."

Lisa glanced up. This was news to her. "You've been doing testing?"

"With one subject." Ted looked slightly chagrined as his glance skipped around the room. "We were already involved in it before we started putting together our best-practices manual."

The manual had simply been a matter of avoiding the impression of lab irregularities. But she also knew that Ted wasn't likely to get into specifics during a regular management meeting. It wasn't as if the head of human resources or maintenance needed to know what innovative research paths they were heading along. They'd learned all too well over the past year how critical data security was.

She couldn't help feeling a buzz of excitement, though.

A new study.

Secure funding.

Her gaze tripped over Rourke's where he was sitting next to Paul at the other side of the table and warmth just seemed to bloom inside her bones.

Yes. Everything was going well.

More than well.

"Sounds good," she said mildly, ducking her head over her notes. "Back to the agenda, then. How many open positions are we still trying to fill?" She looked at the head of H.R., and the meeting proceeded without fanfare, breaking nearly two hours later.

Lunchtime.

The room quickly emptied as she rose from the table. Gathering her things, she watched her husband from the corner of her eyes as he and Ted talked, their voices too low to hear.

"How's married life?" Her brother Paul stopped next to her. "He treating you well?"

"Very." It was the truth, she realized. No matter what his motives were, Rourke did treat her well. They'd had their debates over the past few weeks. Politics. Hockey. Two people with opinions of their own were bound to. But he listened as well as talked. And he didn't judge.

It was a singularly disarming trait.

"You hear about Derek entering that program in Connecticut?"

"Yes." She tapped the end of her pen softly against the table that was striped by brilliant shafts of sunlight cutting through the floor-to-ceiling windows lining the paneled room. "Have you talked to him?"

Paul's lips twisted. "Ramona says I should. She would have lost her mother if it weren't for her finding her half sister to be a bone marrow donor. Now that her mom's finally on the mend, Ramona's more adamant than ever about family sticking together no matter what. But, no, I haven't talked to him."

"Do Mother and Daddy know?"

"I'm sure they do by now. They'll probably end up footing the bill." He sighed. "I'm supposed to believe in healing, but I'm not sure if that twin of mine even feels any remorse. At least Rourke has managed to keep it out of the papers. Only press the institute is getting again is good press. Finally." He suddenly pulled his phone out of his lab coat and checked the display. "I've gotta go. Patient's waiting." He squeezed her shoulder as he headed off.

Lisa looked over at Rourke again. He'd treated *all* of them well. She swallowed the nervousness that wanted to rise in her throat and walked over to him and Ted. "Want to grab some lunch?" The casual question masked the silly trepidation she felt.

Rourke slid his arm over her shoulder in an easy move that nevertheless managed to make her stomach dance a little jig. "Wish I could." His fingers toyed with the bun at the nape of her neck, reminding her all too well of what usually happened when he started pulling the pins out of her hair...where it always seemed to lead. A shiver danced down her spine and the glint in his eyes told her he was well aware of the effect he was having. "But I can't."

She lifted her eyebrows, masking her disappointment. "The boss whose business follows where he wants can't take time to share lunch with his new wife?"

His fingers glided down the nape of her neck. Slipped beneath the collar of her jacket. If she wasn't mistaken, there was actual regret in his eyes. "I've got about ten minutes to spare with Ted—that new thing he's got brewing—and then I'm meeting with the mayor of Boston."

She started. He really *had* had other reasons than her for coming to town. "What for?"

"A construction project." He tilted her head and dropped a kiss on her lips. "Then I need to get back to New York. Cynthia's got my schedule slammed this week."

"You're still going to make it here for the weekend though?" She was painfully aware of Ted standing nearby and the obvious way he was trying not to listen—a physical impossibility, given his proximity—but was more concerned with the possibility that Rourke might *not* be able to return as easily as he'd claimed.

"Oh, yeah, Mrs. Devlin." Rourke glided his finger along the satiny skin of Lisa's neck and watched the flare of her pupils that occurred in direct correlation to his touch.

It was damnably erotic.

"I'll be back." He pressed another kiss to her lips. A kiss that he ended too quickly, but wisely, given their audience and his time constraints.

And then he was striding out of the boardroom, Ted keeping up in his wake before he managed to forget that he *did* have a plate of responsibilities waiting for him, no matter how distracting he was finding his wife to be.

"You haven't told her," Ted asked quietly once they'd reached the privacy of his office. He unlocked a cabinet and pulled out a syringe.

Rourke didn't have to guess what Ted meant. "No reason to tell her."

He shrugged out of his jacket, loosened his belt and turned his back and felt the sting of the injection a few moments later. After several months of having his hip pricked by Ted's needles, the process was done in a matter of seconds and he was fastening his belt again, smoothing down his shirt and pulling on his jacket.

"That's a pretty big secret to keep from the woman you're married to. Think that's wise?"

"You've kept a secret or two yourself," he reminded Ted.

"Not anymore." Ted waved his hand. "Not that I've told Sara Beth that it's your butt I've been having to look at every month," he assured him. "You know that's confidential. But I have told her about the success we're having with the new regimen." He returned to the locked cabinet and retrieved a pill bottle that he tossed to Rourke. "Thirty-day supply. What's the point in keeping it from her? Lisa's a levelheaded woman. She sees situations like this all the time. And she's going to know the details of the treatment as soon as we expand it into an official study."

"She won't have to know that I was patient X." He slid the small bottle into his pocket. The second Taylor had found out it was *he* who was the failure in their baby-making department, she'd gone searching for more fertile pastures. Not that he considered Lisa to be cut from the same cloth as Taylor, but old habits died pretty damn hard.

The only ones who knew about his infertility were Ted—and by necessity his partner, Chance. And the only reason Ted knew was because one night, Rourke hadn't been as closed-mouthed as he usually was, thanks to the deep bottle of whiskey Ted had found him trying to drown himself in the day the divorce had finally become final.

It wasn't one of Rourke's prouder moments, but that particular cloud definitely had its silver lining. Because if he hadn't admitted his problem, there'd have been no reason for Ted to ever tell him about the treatment that he and Chance had already been trying to formulate. Or for Rourke to convince them that he was the perfect candidate to test it on once they believed they were on the right track.

Ted didn't exactly look convinced, but he let the matter drop. "The mayor of Boston, huh?"

Rourke shrugged more casually than he felt. "Just sounding him out on a new multiuse project. There are a couple other locations I'm considering, too."

"But if it were in Boston, you'd have to be around here at least part of the time getting it underway."

"Boston's a good city." He pulled open the door.

Ted grinned. "Particularly when that's where your wife lives, I'd think."

Rourke didn't deny it. He lifted his hand in a brief salute and made his way out of the building before he could fall to the lure of seeking out Lisa just one more time before he left. And it had nothing to do with the faint rattle of pills coming from his pocket.

He'd already become addicted to his cool-facaded wife.

And for the first time in his life, he didn't know what to do about it.

Chapter Eleven

Lisa glanced at the clock on her fireplace mantel.

Nearly eleven o'clock.

Rourke was supposed to have been there hours ago.

She exhaled, staring at the flicker of the two tall candles she'd lit at the center of the dining-room table. Surrounding the crystal candlesticks were baskets of no-longer-warm rolls, a salad that was twenty degrees past wilted and an eggplant lasagna that no longer steamed with an inviting aroma, but was going cold and sunken.

Sexy lingerie and candlelight dinners might be perfect for Sara Beth and Ted. But for Lisa and Rourke, it was turning out to be a foolish endeavor.

First of all, Lisa couldn't cook a decent meal to save her life. Oh, she'd tried. But the first effort was residing in the trash and what sat on the table now was courtesy of her decidedly frantic call to her favorite Italian restaurant.

While she'd been trying to blow out the stench of burned garlic bread from the kitchen, they'd kindly delivered this once-beautiful feast with instructions that even *she* couldn't fail to follow.

And here she sat. Dressed in a filmy black nightie that Sara Beth had positively dared Lisa to buy, candles burned almost down to nubs, and no Rourke in sight.

She was much more annoyed with herself than she was with him. He'd only estimated his arrival when they'd talked that afternoon.

Not even talked.

Texted.

Which was the level that their communications seemed to have sunk to as the week had progressed since he'd shown up at the institute on Monday.

She was the one who'd gone all out with the foolish "welcome home" measures.

Boston wasn't even Rourke's home!

She finally blew out the candles, then rapidly cleared the table. Dumped the food in the trash where it joined the first attempt.

Staring down into the mess, she was appalled to realize there were tears on her cheeks.

She snatched a paper towel from the holder standing on her granite counter and swiped her face. Balled up the paper and pitched it in the trash.

A second later, she whipped the frothy, thigh-length concoction she was wearing over her head and shoved it on top of the food.

Turning on her bare heel, she stomped upstairs to her bedroom and yanked on an old college sweatshirt that reached her knees instead. Then she went into the bathroom and washed her face, twisted the hair that she'd left loose just to please him into a long braid, and went to bed.

She was *not* a lovesick bride and she'd better start remembering it.

Unfortunately, instead of closing her eyes and going to sleep, she lay there, staring at the clock on her nightstand, watching the minutes continue to tick.

That just made her feel weepy again, and after an hour, she finally shoved back the covers and went into the second bedroom that she'd set up as a home office. She sat down at the desk. Her calendar was open.

It was past midnight.

It was official.

They'd been married for four weeks now.

"Happy anniversary." She deliberately flipped the calendar closed. She turned on her computer. Read through a few dozen e-mails, two of which were from her mother about the never-ending details concerning Gerald's upcoming eightieth birthday party.

The light on her message machine was blinking, and she reluctantly hit the button, already braced for "motherly" messages there, as well.

She wasn't disappointed. She buzzed past her mother's voice reminding her that she'd assigned Lisa the duty of hand-addressing the birthday party invitations and tracking the RSVPs and that she'd better start looking for a gown for Paul and Ramona's Christmas Eve wedding, and she skipped past two more messages the second she heard Derek's gruff greetings. She knew that Paul had finally caved to Ramona's insistence that he at least talk to him. All Paul had said about the conversation, though, was that Derek still hadn't apologized for his actions. And until he could do that, Paul wasn't going to waste more time on him. He and Ramona had enough on their plate with their upcoming wedding.

"Hello, Mrs. Devlin." She started at the sound of Rourke's voice coming from the machine. *"I'm running late and you're not answering your cell. See you when I get there."*

"You called," she said to the machine, and just like that, her irritation dissolved, leaving her feeling teary all over again. Acting more like a teenager with her first boyfriend than a grown woman with a career-driven husband, she rewound the message and listened to it a second time.

Then she pulled out her briefcase and unearthed her cell phone that plainly showed her he had called.

Twice.

She dropped the phone on the desk and propped her head in her hands. "You are such a witch, Lisa Armstrong."

"Thought that was *Devlin* now."

She jerked and swiveled in her chair to see Rourke standing there. His jeans were washed nearly white and molded his hips and the thick ivory fisherman's sweater he wore made his shoulders look even broader and his hair even blacker. "How'd you get in?"

"You gave me the security code, remember? I came in through the kitchen." He dropped a very well-used duffel on the floor and stepped into the office, his gaze taking in the tall, mullioned window that overlooked her minuscule backyard, and the old library desk that consumed a good portion of the floor space. "Nice desk."

It was. She'd found it in a consignment shop years ago. "I didn't know you'd called," she said stupidly.

His slashing eyebrows quirked together. "My mother would like to think she raised me better than that. I'm nearly five hours late." He leaned over the chair, propping his hands on the sturdy, wooden arms and brought his head close to hers.

Close enough that she could smell the faint, heady scent of his aftershave.

"Don't you want to know why I was late?"

She was dissolving into a puddle way too easily with this man who'd manipulated her into marriage. "Business, I'm sure." She peeled his hand away from the chair so that she could sidle her way out of the chair past him.

He didn't let go of her that easily, though, and swung her around until she landed flat against his chest. "Yeah. The business of clearing the way to stay here for a few weeks at a stretch, rather than just the weekend."

Her lips parted. "What?"

"I'll make the trip back to New York if I have to, but for now at least, you're going to have to share a drawer or two." His hands slid slowly up and down her back. "So…what do you think?"

Even through her shock she was aware that he sounded diffident.

Which for Rourke was completely out of character.

And that was as alarming as the emotions coiling around inside her. "It doesn't matter what I think. You've already made up your mind, obviously." Made up his mind to change the rules of the game, since they'd already agreed to spend the workweek in their respective cities.

The question was why?

To hasten the chances of her getting pregnant?

His hands slipped down her waist. "I saw the garbage when I came in."

Her cheeks heated. "Dinner was ruined."

"I wasn't talking about the food."

Of *course* he would have to comment on the hank of sheer fabric and ribbon that she'd shoved in alongside the eggplant. "I don't know what you mean," she lied blithely.

He snorted softly, a definite smile hovering around the

corners of his way-too-sexy mouth. "Did you get that thing for me? A little…four-week anniversary gift?"

"Don't be ridiculous." For some reason, it threw her even more that he was aware of that small milestone, too. "I was…was…cleaning out my closet."

"Mmm. And that was the only thing to go."

He clearly didn't believe her. And why would he? She was a pathetic liar.

"Maybe you haven't figured it out, Lisa Armstrong *Devlin*." His hands slid around her waist, bunching up the fleecy sweatshirt. "But I find you insanely sexy. When you're buttoned up in your no-nonsense suits or when you're draped in expensive couture. If wearing a little piece of black nothing makes you feel good about yourself—and what we do together—then have at it. But make no mistake. Even when you look about sixteen, like you do now, you are attractive to me. Hell, all you have to do is simply exist—" she felt the stretched-out hem of the sweatshirt reach her thighs as he continued drawing it upward "—and I want you more than I've ever wanted anything."

"Even children?" She wanted to suck the words back in the second they slid out of her lips. "Don't answer that," she said quickly. There was no need for him to confirm what she already knew.

She was a means to an end for him. Without giving him the child he wanted, he wouldn't have any use for her. And once he did turn her into a mother—which was a state that was preoccupying her thoughts more and more with every passing day—her purpose for him will have been served.

"Fortunately—" he kept slowly bunching the sweatshirt upward and she felt cool air sneak over her bottom "—there's no need to choose." His warm fingers replaced the air, seeming to sear into her bare skin as he lifted her right off her feet. "Did you miss me?"

"I've been swamped at the office," she assured him coolly even while her hands were greedily snaking around his shoulders. "Thanks to your insistence that I be gone for a three-week honeymoon."

His lips twitched. He carried her around the duffel bag on the floor. "Bedroom?"

"End of the hall."

Her town house wasn't huge by any stretch. But it was in a neighborhood that she liked, and it was conveniently located to the institute. So she overlooked the drafty windows and the creaks in the floor, but as he carried her down the short hallway, she was enormously conscious of its shortcomings.

"My place is a lot different than your penthouse," she stated the obvious when he elbowed through the narrow doorway into her dimly lit, chilly bedroom. "Three mornings of waiting for the water heater to kick in will have you running back to New York."

"Don't count on it." He carried her to the shadowy foot of her antique four-poster and slowly lowered her until her bare feet met the braided carpet covering the hardwood floor. "This place smells like you."

There was probably a rulebook somewhere that said she shouldn't be so easily disarmed. But she was, anyway. "And burned garlic bread," she added faintly.

His hands swept beneath the sweatshirt. "Just you," he assured her.

She sucked in a hissing breath when he tugged the garment over her head and his mouth dipped to the naked curve of her shoulder.

"You're shivering," he murmured. "It's cold outside."

The weather had changed. Autumn fully engulfing the city. But the rapidly cooling weather outside that managed somehow to sneak in beyond the brick walls of her town house wasn't what had her shivering now. "That's why I like the fire-place in here." She tugged at his sweater, much more inter-ested in getting her hands beneath to the inferno of his flesh than she was in the temperature outside. "Lift your arms," she finally ordered.

His laugh was muffled in the folds of the sweater as he tugged it over his head and tossed it aside. But before she could press herself up close and personal to that hard, broad chest that she couldn't seem to get enough of, he'd tipped her off her feet again and easily nudged her into the center of her already dis-heveled bed. "Get under the covers. I'll make you a fire."

She scooted back on the mattress, happy enough to do that if he'd just hurry up and join her. "That's what I was kind of expecting," she said pointedly, lifting the blankets in invitation.

His gaze lingered on her bare body for a gratifying moment. Then he seemed to shake himself as he turned toward the fireplace that was in the corner of her bedroom, opposite the bed. "Have you had the chimney cleaned lately?" He crouched down and began pulling wood out of the fire basket next to the hearth, stacking it inside the firebox.

"Every year." Her eyes felt glued to the naked play of muscles as he worked. "It might look old, but we're not going to go up in flames."

He looked at her over his shoulder. "I'm pretty sure we will," he drawled. He shoved some kindling under the stack of wood and pulled out one of the long matches she kept next to the wood.

In seconds, the flame was snapping hungrily at the kindling and he settled the iron screen back in place. Then he rose and turned to face her.

Even though they'd made love dozens of times now, her mouth ran dry as he finished undressing and there was no doubt in her mind as he climbed into the bed and drew her against his fully aroused body that he was interested in anything, just then, other than her. His hands were barely roving over her and she could feel the flames licking at her feet. By the time he pulled her, wet and aching, beneath him and sank so deeply into her that she couldn't help but cry out, she was heading straight for conflagration.

And even as she felt herself spinning wildly out of control, she clung to the fact that in this, at least, he was right there with her.

By the time Lisa woke, the logs in the fireplace were burned down to ash and sunlight was streaming through the twin windows on either side of the bed, shining right across the blanketed bumps of their tangled feet.

She looked at those bumps, feeling the warmth of his feet against hers beneath the blankets, the arm he had planted over her waist, keeping her backside tucked against him, and felt such a wealth of contentment that it was nearly overwhelming.

If she could have blamed it on the unheard-of presence of a man sleeping in her bed, she would have.

But it wasn't just any man.

It was Rourke.

She let out a long breath.

That week at work, she'd worried that having him in her home would feel awkward. It wasn't as if they were a world away in a Mediterranean villa where it had become easy to forget their real world. Their real lives.

This was Boston. Her home. It didn't get much more real than that.

And instead of feeling as if her space was invaded, as if he was taking over another area of her life—particularly knowing that he intended to stay for more than just a few days—she felt…content.

It ought to have confused the life out of her.

But lying there, feeling the steady rise and fall of his chest against her spine, Lisa couldn't summon up even the slightest confusion.

Only contentment.

It was nature itself that finally propelled her out of the warm nest of blankets and Rourke's arms.

The bedroom was at least ten degrees colder than it had been the night before, and she snatched up the first thing her hands encountered to drag over her head as she visited the only bathroom her upstairs possessed. Rourke's sweater.

The soft ivory knit hung over her shoulders and down to her knees and she couldn't help tilting her nose down to smell the scent of him in the weave as she cleaned her face and teeth and worked the remains of her braid out of her hair. A peek through the bedroom door showed her that Rourke hadn't budged since she'd left the bed, except to throw one arm over his head.

His hair—longer now than it had ever been since she'd met him and showing a distinctly unruly wave—was tousled over his forehead. During their honeymoon, she'd gotten used to the sight—as well as the tantalizing feel—of the dark blur of beard that always shadowed his square jaw by morning and for a long moment, she hovered there watching him sleep, a strange sort of tenderness invading her chest.

"If you're gonna stand there staring," his husky voice eventually said, making her start, "come back to bed."

"Men your age shouldn't have so much stamina," she retorted. "And it may be Saturday, but I have important things to do."

He pushed up on his elbow and the bedding fell away from his chest. "Honey, to a healthy guy who isn't quite as old as you seem to think, in the morning, there ain't nothing more important than that."

She forcibly dragged her gaze away from all that male perfection on display and toyed with the too-long sleeves of his sweater that hung below her fingers. "I have to meet my mother and get some stuff for my dad's eightieth birthday party. Evidently, I'm in charge of hand-addressing the invitations and tracking the RSVPs. Making certain that everyone Mother wants there *is* there." Emily would undoubtedly hunt down anyone who didn't respond the way she wanted. All done in the most steely-gracious way, of course.

"Have your secretary do it," Rourke suggested carelessly.

"It's bad enough having my mother push it off on me without even asking if I had the time. I wouldn't dream of pushing this off on Ella. And she'd quickly remind you that she's my administrative assistant."

"Then have Cynthia do it."

"*Your* assistant? You're crazy. She scares me to pieces."

"She's a pussycat."

She hooted. "Maybe to you she is. Besides, she's in New York."

He bunched the pillow beneath his head again. "Then have fun meeting your mom."

Sudden inspiration hit. "You should come with me. Mother actually likes *you*." Emily would be thrilled at the notion that Rourke would be in town for days on end.

He slanted her a glance that gave new meaning to the phrase *bedroom eyes*. "Are you going to make it worth my while?"

"Bribery?" She leaned against the doorjamb. "I'd think a supposedly smitten—" she air-quoted the word "—bridegroom would want to spend every possible moment with his new bride."

"Not when it's under the nose of Emily Armstrong," he returned wryly.

"Ah." She nodded, feeling a smile tug at her own lips, and

crossed her arms. "You *do* really know my mother. Okay. Think of it as a philanthropic gesture. Doing a generous and kind deed for your wife."

He pulled the pillow over his head, lifting his hand in a stopping motion.

"You can't hide from it." She raised her voice. "I've already read about the awards ceremony being held next month and *all* about the noble deeds of this year's award winner." And been dauntingly impressed, wondering how he found the time to invest his *time* as much as his money. He'd not only funded several new shelters in the city, but he'd helped build them. Literally. With hammer and nails. He'd done the same with a new school for girls in Sudan.

But that was what Rourke did. Led by example.

He moved aside the pillow, giving her a baleful look that had her biting the inside of her cheek to hide her delight. It was so refreshing to see the ever-confident man even the slightest bit discomfited. Was it any wonder that she had to take advantage of it?

"If I go with you, will you not say another word about the award business until we actually have to show up at that damn dinner?"

"We?"

"You think I'm going to show up there alone?"

"Won't your family be there? Receiving the award is a big deal."

"Yes, they'll be there," he said, looking aggrieved. "And obviously, so will Nora and Grif."

She hid a smile and drew a cross over her heart. "All right. I promise not to mention it again. Although now I've got to add shopping to the list of things to get done. I assume the thing I'm not supposed to mention will be a formal occasion, and finding a suitable outfit is rarely accomplished in just one day."

"Fine. I'll go with you." His heavy-lidded gaze roved over her. "But first, you have to come here to me."

"I *was* going to fix you some coffee." It was one thing she could prepare faithfully without ruining. She bit the tip of her tongue for a moment. "Strong and hot, just the way you liked it in France."

"Strong and hot, yeah. But the coffee part is not on my mind at the moment."

She knew that. "It is on mine." She smiled slyly and turned to go down the hall.

"Come back here." She heard his footfall on the creaking floorboards followed rapidly by a nasty curse. "Holy— It's *freezing* in here," he yelled.

Not at all his swell Park Avenue penthouse, which undoubtedly even had heated floors.

She glanced over her shoulder and giggled when she saw him coming after her, her grandmother's very faded wedding-circle quilt yanked around his torso. "Don't trip," she warned, dashing to the stairs.

She wasn't fast enough, though. Even hampered by a sixty-year-old quilt, he caught up to her before she reached the landing, scooped her right off her feet, and tossed her over his shoulder.

She found her nose abruptly up close and personal to his quilt-draped backside. "Hey." She wriggled her legs and his arm clamped down over her thighs as he strode back toward the bedroom.

"Caveman." She batted at his butt, but there wasn't much power behind it since she was giggling too hard. Then he flipped her off his shoulder and dumped her, bouncing, onto the bed and she couldn't help but laugh even harder. "What would the business world think if they saw you now?"

"That the caveman wants his woman." His dark eyes were

wickedly intent as he threw aside the quilt and came down beside her, his mouth plundering his way to the valley between her breasts, right through the soft ivory sweater.

Her giggles died as she wrapped herself around him.

But what didn't die was the wistful thought that one day she might actually be his woman. For no other reason than that he wanted *her.*

Chapter Twelve

"**P**retty swell invitations." Sitting across from Lisa two weeks later at the dining-room table in her town house, Sara Beth held up the engraved parchment. "As fancy as a wedding invite." She tucked the invitation carefully into its envelope, added the RSVP card and its little envelope, then handed it off to Lisa.

"Nothing but the best for my mother." Forcing a wry smile, Lisa crossed another name off the list, and started addressing the next envelope, only to have to toss it to the side with the other mis-starts when she began writing the same name that she'd just done. "If she knew I was already a week late getting them out, she'd want to skin me alive. Thanks for giving up your Sunday afternoon to help me, or I'd be even later getting them done." So far, thanks to Sara Beth's help, she'd gotten a quarter of the way through the hundred that were going out.

They'd be going even faster if she could get her mind actually *on* what she was doing.

"Ted's in the lab today anyway." Sara Beth tucked and sealed again, and set the finished envelope down. "It's not like you to procrastinate, though. Even when it comes to your mom. I'm guessing that's because Rourke has kept you pretty busy."

"And even after being back for three weeks, I'm still playing catch-up at the office."

"Again, I'm thinking…Rourke's fault," Sara Beth added dryly. "Good thing he had to make a business trip and give you a break. Where's he off to this time?"

"London. He leaves from New York tomorrow morning." He'd be gone for the week, returning the morning of the awards gala. She was to meet him in New York.

Sara Beth was wagging an invitation between her thumb and forefinger. "Well, I imagine when he gets back, he's going to prefer that your skin is intact."

Lisa managed a smile, but knew it was a miserable effort, particularly when Sara Beth dropped the invitation and reached over the stack of them to pluck the pen out of Lisa's hand.

"All right," she said, no-nonsense written all over her face. "You've been acting weird since I got here. Did you and Rourke have a fight?"

"No." She quickly shook her head and her hair slid over her shoulder. "Rourke's been…fine." Attentive. Passionate. Surprisingly good company even when they weren't in the bedroom.

"Then what's wrong?" Sara Beth nudged the neat stack of invitations and they slid sideways. "Surely you're not letting this stuff really get to you? I know she's your mother, but stressing out about getting these things in the mail a few days late isn't going to accomplish anything." Her lips twisted a little. "Whether they have two weeks' notice instead of three, everyone important enough to be invited is going to be there at Dr. G.'s party."

The invitations weren't Lisa's problem. She pressed her forehead to her hands. "I think I'm pregnant," she blurted.

And had to hold back the sob that wanted to follow on its heels.

She swallowed hard and finally looked up at Sara Beth.

She was watching Lisa with a crinkle between her eyebrows. "*Think?* Have you had a test? How late are you?"

"Well over two weeks, and no. I haven't done a test."

Sara Beth's eyebrows shot up. Not surprisingly. "It'd be pretty easy to run one at the institute," she pointed out.

"Yeah, if I wanted everyone to know my business." Lisa also could have done a test at home if she'd had any privacy in which to do so.

But until that morning when Rourke had flown back to New York, she hadn't *had* a private moment.

"Does Rourke know?" Sara Beth was still clearly trying to gauge the situation. And failing. But how could she not when she didn't know Rourke's real reason for marrying her in the first place?

"No." Her teeth worried the corner of her lip. "I don't want him to until I know for certain."

Sara Beth immediately stood up, and began pulling on the jacket she'd left tossed over the back of Lisa's sofa. "All right, then. Come on. You've got a drugstore nearby. Let's find out for certain."

Lisa didn't budge from her chair.

"Lis?" Sara Beth slowly sat back down. "What's going on? Don't you *want* to be pregnant?"

"The only reason Rourke married me was to *get* me pregnant." It was such a dizzying relief to actually say the words that she barely noticed the tears blurring her vision.

"I'm sure that's not true." Sara Beth's voice was gentle. Calm. "He's crazy about you. Everyone knows that. Even the reporter from that magazine knew that. You're probably just freaking out a little about getting pregnant so quickly. If you're even pregnant at all."

"He didn't invest in the institute because he is crazy about me," Lisa corrected. Her voice was thick. Her throat tight. "He invested in exchange for me giving him the child he wants. Period."

Even with the futile tears burning her eyes, she could see the shock settle over Sara Beth's face. "And you agreed to that?"

"How could I not? The institute would have gone under." Even now, she couldn't bring herself to tell Sara Beth the rest. That Rourke would have seen to it that no other investor would touch them. "Derek's embezzlement went too deep. Rourke knew how precarious things were."

"But nobody at the institute would have expected you to sacrifice yourself to save it!" Sara Beth pushed to her feet and paced the short distance between the dining room and the living room. "I *knew* something wasn't right," she muttered, pacing back again. "I should have listened to my instincts."

"It wouldn't have mattered what your instincts said. I knew what I was agreeing to and I'd…I'd do it again." Lisa wiped her cheeks with the cuff of her sweater, only to realize the sweater wasn't even hers at all. It was Rourke's. She'd pulled it on that morning when she'd gotten out of bed. She hadn't taken it off since.

A fresh wave of tears burned past her lashes.

Sara Beth crouched down next to Lisa's seat. "Then why are you crying?"

"Isn't that what pregnant women do? Cry over nothing?"

"This doesn't feel like nothing to me." She hesitated. "So what is going to happen once you're pregnant?"

Lisa drew in a shuddering breath. "Once the baby's here,

we…we can go our separate ways." That was what they'd agreed to.

"And the baby?"

"Joint custody," she admitted huskily. "If I want to be involved, he won't protest that."

More shock paled Sara Beth's cheeks. "You do, don't you?"

Lisa's arms crossed over her belly. A dim portion of her mind recognized the protectiveness in the gesture. "Yes." She wasn't sure when she'd realized it. But she knew, unquestionably, that she wouldn't be able to hand over her child. *Their* child.

"Oh, Lisa." Sara Beth sighed. "I hate knowing you've been going through this alone. I wish you'd have told me." She pushed back her thick hair as she rose and paced some more. "Actually, what I wish is that Ted had never set up that first meeting between you and Rourke."

"We would never have found another investor like Rourke."

"If I didn't know better, it would sound like you're defending him."

"He's a good man. We…each had something the other wanted. And he's been m-more than fair."

"Oh, my God." Sara Beth stopped next to Lisa's chair. Realization dawned in her eyes. "You're in love with him!"

"I'm…not." But her throat was closing up so tightly, all she could manage was a whisper.

"You are. You're in love with him, and you think once he finds out you're pregnant, that'll be the end of it. That's why you're so upset!"

She opened her mouth to deny it, but nothing emerged.

"Oh, honey." Sara Beth leaned over, wrapping her arms around Lisa in a comforting hug. "It'll be all right. Everything will be okay."

Hadn't Rourke told her that on their honeymoon?

Lisa's tears only came faster. "I don't see how."

Sara Beth looked teary herself when she straightened. She went into the kitchen and came back a moment later, handing Lisa a wad of napkins. "Wipe your eyes." Then with long familiarity, she went to the coat closet by the front door and retrieved Lisa's coat. "You can't hide from this. First thing we need to know is whether or not you are even pregnant. Maybe your period is late because you've been so stressed." She exhaled. "Heaven knows you've had reason to be. First the problems at the institute. Then Derek. Now this."

Lisa slowly took the coat and put it on. She scrubbed her cheeks with the napkins and left them balled-up on the table. "You're right." She hauled in a deep breath. Let it out. She wouldn't know anything until she at least knew that.

"And, you know—" Sara Beth tucked her arm through Lisa's once they were on the sidewalk outside "—even if you are pregnant, who is to say that Rourke will still want you to go your own way? All right, so maybe you didn't go into the marriage with love in your heart, but look where you are now. You won't know unless you talk to him. You're going to New York next weekend for that award thing, right? His feelings could have deepened just as easily as yours."

"That's the romantic in you talking," Lisa said. Even though she'd become guilty of wishing that very thing.

"I just want you to be happy."

"And that's the friend in you talking." Lisa blinked hard, holding another spate of tears at bay. "I don't know what I'd do without you. You're the best friend I could ever have, and all this time, I've been hiding the truth from you. You'd never keep a secret like this from me."

Sara Beth's nose reddened. "Great," she mumbled. "You had to go and say something like that, didn't you."

"What?"

She stopped on the sidewalk and faced Lisa. "You know I love you, right?"

Bewildered, Lisa nodded. "Of course."

"And you know I'd never want to hurt you."

"I know. That's what I was just saying—"

Sara Beth caught Lisa's gloved hands in hers. "My timing stinks." She drew in a deep breath and let it out in a whoosh. "I'm not just your friend, Lisa. I'm…I'm your sister. Your half sister, I mean."

Lisa stared at Sara Beth blankly. A whining siren sounded in the distance. "What?"

"Dr. G. is my father."

Pinpointing, dawning horror closed in on her. She tugged her hands out of Sara Beth's. "Why would you say such a thing?"

Sara Beth looked tormented. "Because I didn't want that secret between us, either!"

"No. Why would you claim you're my father's daughter!"

"Because I am." Sara Beth lifted her gloved hands. "It's not like I planned it. Not even my *mother* planned it."

"You always said your mother used a sperm donor." It had always made sense. Sara Beth's mother, Grace, had practically been her father's first employee. She'd been the head nurse at the institute from the beginning and hadn't retired until Lisa's father had retired.

Grace had never married, but had had a child, thanks to the work of the institute. Lisa knew being the child of artificial insemination had never sat well with Sara Beth, but Lisa had always admired Grace O'Connell's independent style. She'd had a career. A home. A child. She'd lived her life to suit herself.

"Are you saying my *father* was the donor? God, Sara Beth. Hasn't the institute been through the wringer enough? Now you, of all people, are saying he would do something so unethical as switch his own sperm with a donor's?"

"He didn't have to switch anything. He and my mother had an affair. A brief one."

Her entire body tightened with denial. "I don't believe you."

Sara Beth looked as if she wanted to cry. "You've been my best friend our entire lives. Why would I lie about something like that?"

"I don't know." Lisa shook her head, backing away. "My father wouldn't—he *wouldn't* have done that. You're only a month older than I am, for God's sake. That would mean that—"

"I know how bad it sounds."

"Really?"

"I wasn't even planning to tell you," Sara Beth admitted. "To tell any of you. I told your mother I wouldn't and I meant—"

"My *mother!*" Lisa felt like she had the first time she and Sara Beth had ridden a roller coaster at the fair. Sick. And heading for the edge of a rail that would never contain them. "My mother knows?"

"Since I turned fourteen." Tears were on Sara Beth's cheeks now. "That's when your mother stopped liking me."

It made a horrible, awful kind of sense. Until she and Sara Beth had been young teens, Emily had been practically a second mother to Sara Beth. They'd even shared the same nanny when they'd been babies.

But then the day had come when, suddenly, Emily claimed that Lisa needed *new* friends. More suitable friends. Friends of their same class. She'd been hideous and Lisa had snuck out more than once to see Sara Beth. But not until she'd gone to college and had some real freedom had they been able to renew their friendship in full.

"And have *you* known since then?"

"No!" Sara Beth's hands lifted to her sides again. "I only found out earlier this year."

Lisa felt as if she was having an out-of-body experience, watching herself shake her head and back away from the girl who went back to diaper-days with her. She didn't know whether to laugh, or to cry.

How could her father have done such a thing?

"I can't deal with this right now."

"You don't have to deal with anything. Nothing has changed, Lisa. I'm not chomping at the bit to be recognized as an Armstrong. I just…when you talked about secrets…I just wanted you to know. I love you—"

Lisa held up her hand. "Not now." She turned on her heel, running back up the short distance to her front steps.

"Lisa!"

She fumbled with the lock and darted inside, locking the door again behind her.

She heard the pound of feet on the steps, followed by the rap of Sara Beth's knuckles on the door.

"Lisa, come on. Please don't do this!"

It was the coward's way out and Lisa knew it. But just then, she felt incapable of anything else.

She left Sara Beth—her *sister*—knocking on the door and went upstairs. There, she closed herself in her bedroom and she didn't come out again until she was certain that Sara Beth had finally given up.

And gone away.

Rourke stared into the cut-crystal glass of Scotch he held, no closer to drinking it than he'd been when he'd poured the damn thing in the first place.

The New York view that he'd never before tired of was spread out in front of him. The sound system that was the best money could buy was silent. He had a stack of material tossed on the couch beside him that Cynthia had gathered for him, and which he needed to go over before he left for London in the morning, but even that held no interest.

All because of the woman who was his wife.

He sat forward, shoving the drink onto the coffee table, and pushed to his bare feet to pace the length of his living room. The floor here sure in hell wasn't cold like the floor at Lisa's. But after the two weeks he'd just spent there in Boston with her, he'd gotten used to that shocking contact every time he left the warmth of her bed.

Now, he had one of the biggest international deals of his life to prepare for, and all he could think about was getting back to that warmth.

He raked his fingers through his hair. Pressed the heels of his palms against his eyes.

It wasn't even just the sex. It was *her.*

But they had a deal. A deal of his own freaking making. And even if he had the guts to change the terms of the deal, why would she want to once she knew the whole truth about him and her sacred institute?

He muttered an oath, returned to the couch and snatched up the top file. But when the doorbell chimed a short while later, he was no more interested in the contents than he'd ever been.

He tossed it aside and went to the door. Cynthia was supposed to deliver one more report from his legal department, but he'd figured she wouldn't get it to him until morning. He yanked open the door.

It wasn't his wholly efficient and cantankerous assistant at all. It was his wife. As if he'd conjured her there by his thoughts, alone.

He frowned. She had circles under her eyes and her lips were practically colorless. "Lisa. What's wrong?"

"I didn't know where else to go."

The admission sent a jolt through him. He took her arms

and pulled her inside. "You're not even wearing a coat." Just a familiar-looking ivory sweater that nearly drowned her to the knees of her narrow blue jeans.

She looked down at herself, as if surprised. "I...I guess I forgot it on the plane." Then she chewed the inside of her cheek and warily looked around him. "Are...are you alone?"

His jaw tightened. She knew his body almost as well as he did; and he, hers. But she trusted him so little that she had to ask such a question? "It's nearly midnight. Who would I be with?"

Her lashes fell. "I don't know. I'm sorry." She shook her head and the strands of hair falling out of her messy knot clung to her cheek. "I found out today that my father had an affair," she said baldly.

He swallowed an oath, his frustration fizzling. "No wonder you look shell-shocked." He steered her from the foyer into the living room. "Sit." He shoved aside the mountain of paperwork on the couch. "I'll get you something hot to drink."

She was still sitting there, staring at the unadorned windows, when he returned. "Here." He closed her cold hands around the thick, white mug as he sat down on the coffee table in front of her. "Drink. It's coffee and probably too strong."

She lifted the mug. Took a ginger sip and winced. "Really strong."

"It's been sitting on the burner a while," he admitted. Ignored just as much as his Scotch had been. "Now, talk."

She drew in a deep, shuddering breath. "My father had an affair with Grace O'Connell. Sara Beth's mother. About twenty-nine years ago. Supposedly it ended almost as quickly as it began." She twisted the mug back and forth between her fingers. "He, um, he worked with her. She was the head nurse at the institute for years."

"How'd you find out about this now?"

"Sara Beth told me." Her jaw flexed. "Turns out that she's my sister and I accused her of lying to me."

"Obviously, she wasn't."

She shook her head. Looked upward and blinked hard. "I went to my parents. I didn't even need to see the guilt on my father's face. All I had to see was the iciness on my mother's." She looked at Rourke and the pain in her eyes made him ache. "Oh, God, I don't want to be like her."

He took the mug from her hands and set it aside. "Your mother isn't all bad." He closed his hands around hers, rubbing heat into them. "She raised you."

"Right. She raised Derek, too, and look how well *that* turned out."

His thumbs moved in circles against her wrists. He couldn't think about Derek. Not without thinking about his own secrets. "And Paul," he reminded her. "And Olivia."

"And she ostracized Sara Beth, who didn't do anything to deserve it. I don't know who to blame. My mother for driving him to another woman, or my father, for being so—" She shook her head. "I can't even come up with a word for it."

"Imperfect?" Rourke kept his voice mild. "Honey, don't forget that this all happened before you were born. What bothers you more? The fact that your best friend is not just a sister of your heart? Or the fact that she's proof that your father is more human than saint?"

"I don't know." She folded forward, pressing her forehead to her wrists.

His hands moved from hers to cradle her head, his fingers tunneling gently through her hair, loosening it from the band that wasn't doing a very good job. "It was a long time ago. And it has nothing to do with the way he was a father to you."

"And not a father to Sara Beth at all," she mumbled. "The only thing he did was ensure that when she retired, Grace was financially set."

"Did she want more than that?"

"She refused to take any sort of support from him. But he should have done better." She looked up. "Why don't you ever talk about *your* father?"

"The only thing that made Jack Devlin my father was his DNA." Rourke sat back. His voice was even. Entirely devoid of emotion. "He was a bastard and when he decided he wasn't interested in being a husband or a father, he locked us out of our own home and that was that. There's no point in talking about someone who, as far as I'm concerned, doesn't even exist."

"And your sisters?"

"Feel the same way."

"I'm sorry."

"Be sorry for my mother. She's the one who had to fight just to keep us all together."

"She did a tremendous job. Look at you." She didn't have to gesture to their palatial surroundings to make her point. It was evident in the man he was.

While she sat there, having denied her best friend and hiding the fact from her husband that she was very likely pregnant.

Maybe she was worse than her mother.

She stared at Rourke, the words that would probably have him routing out the manager of the nearest baby store to open it up for him, even if it was the middle of the night, jamming in her throat.

"Hey." He ran his thumb down her cheek. "It will work out."

That was what everyone seemed to keep saying. But he didn't know what she suspected.

"You've been friends with Sara Beth a lot longer than you've known she's your half sister," he went on. "You'll get past the shock. You'll talk. If the fights my own sisters have are any indication, you'll end up closer than ever when the dust is settled."

Her nose prickled. Her eyes burned. This man who'd manipulated her into marriage was way too good for her. "I'm…I mean I think I—" Her voice strangled to a halt.

"I think you just need a break." He pulled her to her feet, and she was too numb to resist. "Stay here for a few days if you need to. You'll have plenty of peace and quiet since I'll be leaving in the morning. You'll let the shock settle and you'll head back into it with everything you've got, just like you always do."

She looked up at him.

He was the same man whose intensity had been as captivating as it had been terrifying.

"Make love to me," she whispered.

His sharp gaze went even sharper and afraid that he'd see too much and what he'd see would be found wanting, she pressed herself against him. Slid her hands up into the thick, slippery black silk of his hair. "Right here." She brushed her lips over his earlobe. When the heels of her boots hit the floor again, she caught the way his lashes had lowered. The way his jaw was flexed. "Right now."

His hands closed around her waist. Slid up her spine. Down again. "Is this my sweater?"

"Yes."

A faint, low sound seemed to rumble around his chest.

And then his mouth was on hers and the taste of him filled her senses.

She was reeling when he finally lifted his head. His fingers twisted through hers and he led her through the penthouse until they reached his bedroom. And there, he undressed her slowly. Carefully. As if she were a precious package to be unwrapped.

And then when he was as bare as she, when there was nothing between them but her secret and he pressed her back onto the bed and his lips found hers again while his hands began playing her like a delicate instrument, she knew that whatever the future held, when it came to Rourke and her heart, she was utterly lost.

Chapter Thirteen

"Do you remember the first time we danced?"

"How could I forget the Founder's Ball?" Lisa kept a pleasant smile on her face in honor of the photographer who stood to one side of the dance floor, capturing Rourke's image for posterity.

They were the first of the couples ceremoniously circling the dance floor in the Grand Ballroom of the Waldorf Astoria. Dinner had been served, speeches delivered, and Rourke—disarmingly deprecating over the honor—had received his philanthropic award.

The crystal globe signifying his worldwide efforts was now waiting at their empty table.

"It was the *only* time we danced," she reminded him.

Until now. And eight weeks of marriage to the man didn't make him any less disturbing to her senses.

If anything, he was more so, now that she knew for certain she was carrying his child.

While he'd been in London and she'd been essentially hiding out in his penthouse, she'd finally taken a home pregnancy test. Twice.

There was no question that she was pregnant.

"You looked very beautiful that night." His voice drew her thoughts out of darkness, the way it always seemed to. "As I recall, not thrilled that I'd crashed the party, though."

"And you were very objectionable that night." She managed a dulcet smile. "As I recall."

His lips twitched. His hand drifted dangerously low over the back of her black column dress. "Verbal sparring with you is almost as much fun as—"

"Don't even say it," she warned. "Not when your mother is dancing three yards away from us with Griffin Harper." Grif's wife, Nora, was sitting at one of the round crystal-laden banquet tables chatting with Rourke's sisters.

"As beautiful as you were that night—" he pressed his mouth close to her ear "—you're even more so tonight. But I can't wait to get you out this dress."

Anticipation dripped through her, measured equally by anxiety. That was what happened when you were afraid to tell your husband that his heart's desire had come true.

Her fingers trembled as they grazed over the fine black wool covering his shoulder. "We can't leave yet. You, um, you should dance with Nina and your sisters."

"That's nowhere near as much fun."

An unexpected smile hit her lips. "I hope not."

But almost as if he'd heard them, Griffin danced next to them. "Shall we change partners?"

Rourke gave her a look that had her nerve endings dancing as he handed her off to the older man, and took his mother sedately across the dance floor.

"I think we could power the city for a few nights on the

energy you two give off," Griffin commented. "It's obvious you're very happy together."

Lisa just smiled, not quite knowing how to respond to that. "This is quite an event you put on here."

"In this world, it seems we have to shell out money to bring even more in." He smiled ruefully. "Nora considers this quite a dog and pony show. Hates it more every year."

Lisa glanced toward his wife. "How is she feeling?"

His smile dimmed a little. "As well as we can expect. Fortunately, she still has more good days than bad."

Lisa could hardly bear it that this man was so in love with his wife, but was going to lose her in the end. "I'm glad to have this opportunity to see you both again."

Griffin chuckled. "Oh, my dear, as time passes, you'll probably get heartily tired of us popping in and out of your and Rourke's lives."

Her throat went tight. Her time in Rourke's life as his wife would be up all too soon.

She forced a smile and shook her head. "Nobody could get tired of either one of you."

Fortunately, the orchestra was concluding their song, and taking advantage of the break, Lisa excused herself, taking a quick break to the ladies' room where she managed, by dint of a little blush and gloss, to look much livelier than she felt. She adjusted one of the tiny, sparkling pins that held her mass of waves away from her face and brushed her hands down the front of her dress. Aside from the bodice fitting more snugly across her bust, there was no visible evidence of the changes going on inside her.

But she wasn't so confident that would be true once Rourke had her wearing nothing at all.

She returned to the ballroom where the orchestra was in full swing again, and Rourke was on the dance floor with

Tricia. His sisters and their spouses were dancing, too, and she returned to her seat at their empty table.

She traced the golden imprint of Rourke's name on the base of the globe-shaped award.

Who was this man she'd married?

Generous philanthropist.

Powerful, corporate Midas.

Father of the baby growing inside her.

Man whom she'd impossibly fallen for.

"Excuse me, Mrs. Devlin?"

She looked up to see a young, petite blonde standing next to the table. "Yes?"

The girl smiled, looking vaguely familiar, and held out her hand. "I'm Victoria Welsh. I'm, well, I'm—"

"Ramona's sister," Lisa inserted. Of course, the resemblance was to her brother's fiancée. She was ridiculously grateful to have something else to focus on and she clasped the other woman's hand.

Victoria smiled faintly. "Yes. I'm afraid that fact still seems strange to me, even after all these months."

Lisa could well imagine. Victoria had been conceived using donor eggs through the institute. Ramona had been desperate to find a donor for her gravely ill mother, and it had forced her to use extraordinary tactics to find one when she'd learned her mother had once donated eggs to the institute. "I know how grateful Ramona is to you. And her mother, too." Not only had Ramona found Victoria, but she'd fallen in love with Paul. And Lisa knew her brother had never been happier.

Victoria waved a slender hand. "I'm just glad I was a suitable donor match for Katherine," she dismissed. "Finding a family I didn't even know I had is…quite remarkable. But I don't want to intrude on your evening. I just wanted to say hello. I know you're going to be Ramona's sister-in-law once she and Paul get married."

"Christmas Eve. You'll be there, won't you?" She knew that Ramona was hoping so.

"I'm planning on it." The younger woman tucked a lock of pretty blond hair behind her ear. She glanced toward one side. "I'd better get back to my date, though." She rolled her eyes a little. "An old friend, but if he gets bored, I'm afraid his hands will start wandering to one of the servers."

"Then you can do better," Lisa advised.

"Oh, we're not serious." Victoria's gaze went to the dance floor for a moment. "There just needs to be more men around like your husband." She smiled again. "Enjoy the rest of your evening and please tell Ramona that I said hello."

"I will." Lisa watched the girl gracefully weave through the tables until she reached a sulky-looking guy about her own age.

"Do you know Victoria Welsh?" Nora Harper slipped into the chair beside her. She looked brilliant in a royal-blue gown that set off her striking, silver hair. "The Welsh family have always been such good supporters of the foundation."

"I've just met her tonight."

"Ah. Well, she was always such a sweet child." Nora gently squeezed Lisa's bare arm. "Have you been enjoying yourself?"

"It's a lovely event. And the setting—" She lifted her shoulders. "I can't imagine any location being more beautiful."

"It is quite grand." Nora watched the dancers circling around the floor. "Though, honestly, next year I'm going to insist that Griffin get a more lively orchestra. All we've heard tonight have been waltzes." She gave Lisa such a mischievous look that she couldn't help but smile. "Bo-ring."

"I think everyone here figures it's classic," she confided softly.

"How tasteful of you, dear." Nora patted her arm again. "Now go rescue your husband and take him out of here."

"But it's still early." Rourke was pretty much the guest of honor. It was a much better excuse than that she was afraid he would realize sooner rather than later what she hadn't told him since those little pregnancy test sticks had turned pink.

"Nonsense." Nora waved that off. "You're newlyweds. Anybody who expects you to hang around a stodgy awards dinner like this has just forgotten what it feels like to be young and in love."

Young and in love.

The phrase circled in Lisa's mind.

It might describe her, but she knew it didn't describe Rourke.

And how badly she wished that it did. If he loved her, they could have a future together. A real future. A real family instead of legal documents and visitation rights.

But she didn't argue with Nora. She knew full well that Rourke was anxious to get out of there, and with Nora watching so benevolently, she didn't have any logical alternative.

So she wound her way through the dancers and patted Tricia on the shoulder, forcing a cheerfulness that she was eons from feeling. "Can I play fast and easy with traditional roles and cut in?"

Tricia grinned, quickly surrendering her brother. "Be my guest. Rourkey hasn't talked about anything but you, anyway." She winked and hurried off the dance floor.

"Couldn't stay away?" Rourke pulled her back into his arms.

It was more true than he knew. "I have permission from the hostess herself that you've been such a good boy, you can now be excused from the dinner table."

"Thank God. I've never hated traveling so much as I have this past week." His grin was decidedly unboyish as he immediately stopped dancing and herded her toward the nearest exit.

"What about your award?"

"My mother will grab it," he assured her. "And add it to the wall of shame at the house."

"I need my coat," she reminded him when it seemed as if he intended to forget that fact, too, in his rush to escape.

He veered the other way. Stopped at the coat check and gave the girl a tip along with the stub. Two minutes later, he was swinging her cashmere cape around her shoulders and they were on their way out into the chilly night air.

He didn't even bother to call for his driver, but hustled her into the first cab that came by. "Some people might consider your hastiness very unseemly," she pointed out.

"I don't have designs on some people," he returned.

She smiled faintly and rubbed her palm against his and felt the faint clink of her wedding ring against his. "It's been a perfect evening," she admitted softly. "I wish I didn't have to go back to Boston tomorrow." For that entire week, she'd hidden out in Rourke's penthouse, doing her work as best she could from the safe distance of knowing she didn't have to face Sara Beth, or anyone else.

"You still haven't talked with Sara Beth."

Lisa's throat tightened. "No."

"It's only going to get harder the longer you let it go."

"Anxious for me to go home?"

His hand tightened around hers. "No. As far as I'm concerned, you can just stay here."

There was an intensity in his voice that made her heart catch. "I've played coward long enough. I know that as well as you. And I can't let it keep getting in the way of work. I need to pull my own weight there."

"You don't *have* to work."

"The institute is who I am."

"Who you are is my wife." His thumb ran along her wrist.

Pressed against the pulse that was fluttering uncontrollably. "Being the administrator there is what you do."

"It's my career." She was reminding herself just as much as him. "It's important to me."

"And you're important to me."

Her mouth went dry.

Even in the dim light of the cab, she could see the seriousness in his gaze. "Because of the agreement we have." It was a wonder he couldn't hear the ponderous thudding of her heart.

"Because of you."

She couldn't breathe. "Rourke—"

"Meter's still running, folks."

She blinked, realizing the cab had stopped in front of Rourke's building. Even Rourke had seemed oblivious to that fact.

He paid the driver and stepped out of the cab, holding her hand to help her out.

She had a dizzying flashback to the day of their wedding, when she'd stepped out of the limousine almost in this exact spot.

He'd kissed her, crushing her bouquet of flowers. The photograph that had caught them at that moment was still being splashed all over the news outlets, blasting their "fairy-tale" marriage.

And how true that fairy-tale term was.

Because fairy tales didn't come true.

"Lisa?" Rourke's hands closed over her shoulders. "You all right?"

She stared into his face. "I need to tell—"

"Lisa."

She jerked away from the hand that touched her from behind, sinking deeper against Rourke's chest even as she recognized the man who'd spoken. "Derek," she gasped.

He looked terrible.

Always thinner than the more athletically built Paul, he looked more like a walking skeleton than the brother she knew. His dark hair had unfamiliar strands of silver in it, there were sunken circles beneath his brown eyes, and his coat looked as if it was barely hanging on his frame.

"Armstrong. What the hell are you doing here?" Rourke was tucking her practically behind him.

But Derek wasn't so easily waylaid. He angled to the side, his eyes fastened on Lisa. "I've been watching the building all night waiting for you. I've been calling you for months."

Rourke shifted. Blocking Derek again. "And she hasn't called you back. Take the hint."

"Stay out of this, Devlin. This is between me and my sister."

"You mean my *wife*," Rourke reminded him and there was such loathing in his voice that it penetrated even Lisa's shock.

"That's right. Your wife." Derek suddenly focused on Rourke. "Is that why you don't want me to talk to Lisa so badly? I'm sure you're the one who's kept her from returning my calls. Or haven't you told her about our history?"

"The only thing I care about is you upsetting Lisa." Rourke's voice was flat. Deadly.

She avoided the arm he was using to shield her from Derek. "Rourke hasn't kept me from anything. What history?"

Derek shot her a glance. "I just needed to talk to you. Try to explain. Tell you I was sor—"

"*What* history!" Her voice rose. Even Louis, the doorman of Rourke's building, gave her an alarmed look from across the wide sidewalk. And she could see Tom, the intimidating night security guard, striding through the well-lit lobby toward the door.

Rourke's hands closed over her shoulders. "It's old news. It doesn't matter anymore."

"Right." Derek's face tightened. "When Taylor left you, you said there'd be a day I'd live to regret it."

"Taylor!" Her stomach clenching hard, Lisa looked from Rourke to Derek and back again. "What about your ex-wife?"

"Well?" Derek glared at Rourke. "Are you going to tell her or not?"

She twisted out from beneath Rourke's hands. "Tell me what?"

Rourke's jaw was practically white. "It has nothing to do with us—"

"Taylor had an affair with me," Derek inserted flatly. "We met when she was coming to the institute six years ago, trying to get pregnant with the kid *he* wanted."

Lisa's head felt light. Her stomach dipped woozily.

"Only it turned out that *she* wasn't the one with the problem," Derek added. His gaze was on Rourke again. "Did you want to get back at the institute for discovering the fact that you were shooting blanks all along, or did you just want to get back at me because Taylor decided she preferred my bed to yours?"

"She must not have preferred it for long," Rourke said curtly. "Judging by how quickly she moved on from it. She'd dumped you even before the ink on our divorce decree dried."

"Rourke's not infertile," Lisa inserted faintly.

Derek's lip curled, not listening to her any more than Rourke was. "But you never got over it, did you? You took the first chance that came along to get your revenge. You married my sister. You sank so much money into the institute we might as well take down the Armstrong part and put up Devlin in its place."

"And why did the institute need the money in the first place?" Rourke wasn't quite as tall as Derek, but he was far more powerfully built. And when he took a step toward Derek, her brother actually took a step back.

It didn't seem possible that they could come to blows but Rourke's hands were fisted and so were Derek's.

Lisa's mind was reeling, but she quickly wormed her way between them. "Stop it!"

"Stay out of the way." Derek's hand started to push her to one side.

"Don't touch her." With one arm, Rourke scooped her out of the way as he planted his other hand on Derek's chest. He shoved him back a solid two feet.

Derek caught himself from stumbling and advanced again. "You think I want to hurt her? She's my sister! I'm not the one using her to get back at me," he reminded him.

He finally looked at Lisa. "Yeah. I've made some mistakes. Big ones. But I'm finally getting help and facing my gambling and the drugs. I've been in rehab for the past two months. I'm trying to make things right again. While *he*—" he jerked his head toward Rourke "—is just using the situation for revenge.

"He warned me then that I'd live to regret crossing him. I never believed he'd wait all these years to prove it. But now he's got you shackled to him. Probably convincing you to stay away from the institute, even. Keep you busy so you wouldn't notice him taking it over right under our noses!"

"Stop." Lisa covered her ears, though it didn't stop the sounds of everything crumbling around her. Nausea rose in her throat and she struggled to stop it. "You're not part of the institute anymore, Derek. You gave up that right when you nearly ruined us!"

"Everything all right, Mr. Devlin?" The security guard, looking very uptight and very large, stopped next to them. His hand was on his radio, almost as if he wished it were a weapon. "If this guy's bothering you, I can—"

"It's fine, Tom." Rourke didn't take his eyes off Lisa's

brother, not trusting him for a second. It was taking everything he possessed not to pound his fist into the other man's face and only the fact that the weasel *was* Lisa's brother was preventing him from doing just that. "Go back inside."

Tom gave Derek a hard glare, but he finally turned on his heel and returned to the building. He didn't go inside, however. Just stopped at the doorway next to Louis and folded his arms across his chest, clearly intending to bar Derek from the building, if the need arose.

"How'd you know I was in New York?" Lisa's face was pale and pinched.

"Ella told me." Derek made a face. "She said you'd been here for the past week."

"Paul knew."

"I wanted to see you first. Before I saw Paul."

Lisa swayed as if the words were a physical blow and Rourke tried to reach for her again, but she held him off just as surely as she was keeping away from her brother.

His gut tightened. He should have told her everything. He'd known it and now it was too late. She'd never believe him now. "Princess, don't let him get to you."

She fastened her glittering gaze on him. "Then tell me none of it is true." She made a visible effort to stop her lips from trembling. "Tell me he wasn't the one your wife cheated on you with. That you and Taylor were never involved at the institute before now."

He wished he could. And not because of Taylor, he knew. But because of the pain on Lisa's face.

Her lips twisted at his silence. "So. That's what it was all really about." A tear slid down her cheek, catching the light from the streetlamp as clearly as a diamond.

And the sight of it cut through him as surely as glass.

He took a step toward her. "No, that's not what this is about."

She gave him a disbelieving look. "You didn't find a whole lot of satisfaction knowing that it was *his* sister who was going to have to give you the child you wanted?" She waved at her brother. "The child your ex-wife didn't give you?" Her voice cracked.

"More like the child he *couldn't* give her," Derek corrected, cuttingly. "That's what they learned at the institute." He gave Rourke a goading look. "Taylor wanted me to get her pregnant, you know. As soon as the test results came back confirming that you couldn't cut it, she even suggested burying the results. Said she could pass the baby off as yours. Seeing as how the kid would probably be your only heir." His lips twisted. "All that money to inherit. It was the one thing about you that she really didn't want to give up."

Lisa's hand flashed out and she slapped her brother's face.

Derek slowly lifted a hand to the red mark she'd left on his cheek. He looked pained. "Lisa, I just wanted you to know the truth. I'm not trying to hurt you."

"No," she said thickly, "you've done enough of that, already, haven't you? And not just me. But Paul and…and everyone else at the institute. We would have had to close our doors if not for Rourke."

"Are you really going to paint him as some hero?"

Lisa laughed, but there was no humor in it. Only a deep dark pain that made Rourke ache inside, knowing that Derek wasn't the only reason it was there.

Rourke was responsible for plenty of it.

"Everybody has had secrets," she told them both. Or neither one in particular. "But they always come out." She looked at Derek. "If you're really trying to get better, then I…I wish you luck. But as far as what went on with you and Taylor and the institute, obviously, someone was mistaken about Rourke."

She slanted her gaze to Rourke. More diamond-sharp tears

glittered on her lashes. "Otherwise, I wouldn't be pregnant with your baby now, would I?"

Her words jerked through him. "You're pregnant?"

Her chin lifted. "Yes. So we can put an end to this whole charade even sooner than I'd hoped."

His hands went out toward her, but she sidled out of his reach, holding the folds of her cape closely, protectively, around her body.

"There was no mistake." Derek's voice reminded Rourke that he was still there. "I saw the test results, myself. Dr. Adams was on staff then. He met with Rourke and Taylor after hours. Kept everything nice and hush-hush and off the books so nobody would suspect that the Midas-boy and his beautiful wife were having trouble in the baby department. Rourke couldn't have gotten anyone pregnant."

Rourke eyed the other man. He'd always wondered how he'd feel, facing the man who'd been the final ruination of his marriage to Taylor, and knew the murderous anger inside him now had nothing to do with old history. It had everything to do with the here and now. With the fear of losing the woman he'd never expected to love. "I'm going to give you twenty seconds to get the bloody…hell…out…of… here."

"I'm not leaving until Lisa tells me to go."

Lisa looked straight at him. "Go."

Rourke could almost have felt a little sorry for the man if he weren't so close to wanting to kill him.

Derek's face fell. He nodded. "For what it's worth, Lis, I am sorry." Then he turned on his heel, holding his coat close around his skinny body, and disappeared around the corner of the building.

Lisa looked at Rourke. "You're the subject in Ted's study." There was no question in her voice. Only realization.

His hands curled at his sides. The truth. But it was too little. And way too late. "Yes."

She pressed her lips together. Her lashes swept down, hiding her eyes. Another gleaming tear was slowly creeping down her cheek. Her shoulders moved.

Then she suddenly lifted her head. Swiped her hand down her cheek. No longer was there an ocean of warmth in her eyes. No pain. No…anything.

Except ice.

"Then I guess you and Doctors Bonner and Demetrios all have reason to celebrate." She swept her cape more securely around her and looked over her shoulder toward the door. "Louis—" she raised her voice so the doorman could hear "—would you please hail a cab for me?"

"Yes, ma'am." Louis grabbed his whistle and headed toward the curb.

Rourke wanted to grab her. Keep her from going. But he feared that if he did, she would shatter. And he had nobody but himself to blame. "Where are you going?"

She didn't so much as look at him again. "Home."

Chapter Fourteen

"All right." Lisa tucked her pen back into her portfolio and looked around the boardroom table at the members of institute's management team gathered there. "Thank you all for coming this morning. Let's all have a good week." She smiled as everyone began filing out of the meeting, though she felt nothing.

Had felt absolutely nothing since every hopeful dream she might have felt where her marriage was concerned had died an ugly death on the cold sidewalk outside of Rourke's beautiful apartment. She hadn't cared about the curious looks her formal gown had gotten when she'd managed to catch a late plane home to Boston. Hadn't been interested in the lights blinking on her message machine when she'd let herself into her chilly, dark town house.

When that morning had rolled around and she'd automatically prepared for work, arriving at the institute well before it opened, she hadn't even worried whether or not she might run into Sara Beth.

Her body was on autopilot. Anything but focusing on what needed to be done at the institute was cordoned off in another part of her brain.

And that was just the way Lisa wanted it.

"You going to sit in here all morning and stare at the walls?"

She blinked and looked toward the doorway. Sara Beth was standing there, wearing a pair of deep blue scrubs.

Lisa folded her portfolio with a snap and pushed out of her chair. She headed to the door, prepared to walk past Sara Beth, but Sara Beth stepped right in her path. "I'm not going to let you avoid me forever," she said bluntly.

"I'm not avoiding you."

Sara Beth's eyebrows shot up. "Could have fooled me." Her gaze was assessing. "You look terrible."

"Blame it on morning sickness."

Sara Beth's lips parted softly. "You *are* pregnant." She couldn't seem to help herself as she touched Lisa's arm. "Do I give you congratulations, or—"

"Congratulate your husband and Dr. Demetrios." Lisa stopped her before she could bring up Rourke. "Since they're the ones responsible for it. If either one of them had been present at our management meeting, I would have congratulated them myself."

Sara Beth's brows drew together. "What are you talking about?"

"Ted hasn't told you?" A tremble entered her voice and Lisa quickly plugged the trickle in the emotions she'd carefully dammed away. "About the study he and Chance have been working on?"

"You mean the sperm motility thing?"

"Rourke's been the study subject. If their success with him

can be replicated, Bonner and Demetrios are going to make this institute famous all over again."

"Lisa." Sara Beth caught her arm as she slipped past her. "I swear to you. I didn't know Rourke was the one."

"That makes two of us." She started to turn away, only to stop. "About the stuff I said—"

"You were upset," Sara Beth said quickly. "And my timing couldn't have been worse."

"The timing shouldn't have mattered." She mentally shoved a fist into another trickle. "I know you were just trying to be honest. If anything, we all should be taking lessons from you in that regard."

"That's not true," Sara Beth dismissed. "What about Rourke? You've told him?"

"Yes." The trickle was in danger of becoming a deluge. She deliberately stepped away from Sara Beth, aiming blindly for the elevator down the hall. "I've got to get back to my office. I have a conference call in a few minutes." It was a bald lie. She wouldn't know what was on her calendar if she'd had it opened in front of her.

"What did he say?" Sara Beth trotted after her.

"There was nothing for him to say." Not even with Sara Beth, not even now, after all the secrets, the half-truths, could she bring herself to tell her what part she'd really played in Rourke's plan. She jabbed her finger viciously into the call button and the elevator doors immediately slid open. "He wanted an heir. He's getting one."

Sara Beth stepped into the elevator with her. "You didn't tell him you loved him."

Lisa looked up at the floor display above the door. The numbers wavered, like a wave of heat was shimmering in front of them. She blinked. The shimmer disappeared. "No point.

I know exactly what Rourke wants." Her crisp voice cracked. "It is *not* me."

"Then he's a fool," Sara Beth said quietly. "What can I do?"

Another trickle broke through the dam. Lisa shored it up as best she could. "Just…be my friend."

Sara Beth nodded. Her eyes were moist but her gaze was steady. "Always."

Lisa smiled shakily. "Be my sister."

Sara Beth's nose turned pink. "Always." She reached out. Caught Lisa's hand and squeezed it.

A faint sob sneaked out of Lisa's throat. She coughed, trying—failing—to cover it.

Sara Beth laughed, just as brokenly. "What, um, whatever happened to the birthday invitations?"

The elevator reached the first floor and Lisa dashed her hand over her cheeks, stepping out. The waiting room beyond the receptionist's desk was already full of patients. "I dumped them back on my mother's desk to deal with."

Sara Beth looked surprised. "Well." A dimple flirted in her cheek. "Good for you."

"Yeah. Except it'll be all my fault if nobody shows up at the birthday party for Dad—" She broke off.

"It's okay," Sara Beth assured her.

Lisa exhaled. "Only because you are extraordinary."

"Stop." Sara Beth slid her finger beneath her lashes. "You'll make my mascara run and we've got a load of patients today. D'you, um, want to meet for lunch?"

It was such an ordinary thing. That meant so very much. Lisa nodded, unable to speak.

And Sara Beth seemed to know it. "I'll swing by your office then," she said.

Lisa nodded. She turned quickly to get back *to* her office before the dam could burst entirely and she'd start bawling in the corridor where anyone and their mother's brother could witness the flood.

But as she turned, the overhead lights seemed to tilt alarmingly. And all she could do was say "Sara Beth?" as the ground slid sideways and she went right along with it.

"She's coming around now."

Lisa groaned, pressing her hand against the throbbing pain at the back of her head. She opened her eyes and found herself surrounded. Paul. Chance. Sara Beth. Even Wilma, the institute's devoted receptionist, was hovering over her, looking worried. "What happened?" Her fingers gingerly felt around the knot on her head.

"You fainted," Sara Beth said.

"Nearly gave me a heart attack," Wilma added. "One minute you were standing there. The next we all heard your head cracking against the floor."

"Speaking of which," Paul said, "an ice pack would be good."

"I'll get it." Wilma hurried out of the room and Lisa realized they were all crowded into one of Chance's examining rooms.

She worked her arms behind her, trying to sit up, but Paul held her in place with a firm hand on her shoulder. "Just be still for a while longer." He flashed a penlight over one of her eyes. Then the other. "You hit your head pretty hard."

"I'm fine now." She stared at the ceiling lights over his head. No wavering. No nauseating shifting.

"Sara Beth told us you're pregnant." Her brother eyed Chance. "Dr. Demetrios is going to examine you. Just to be safe."

"All I did was get a little dizzy. And I know how busy Chance's schedule is without having to slide me in, too."

"I think he'll manage. Don't be a bad patient," Paul advised, his lips tilting. "Sets a bad example." He stepped out of the way. "Let me know what you find," he told Chance as he left.

Her brother was a fine doctor, but she was glad that he wasn't the one planning to examine her. She looked up at Sara Beth and Chance. "I really don't want to make a fuss."

"It's here or the hospital," Chance said. "Your choice." He smiled faintly when she made a face.

"Here you go, dear." Wilma hurried in with an instant ice pack that she was already shaking to activate. She handed it to Lisa and quickly exited again.

"Help her get into a gown," Chance advised, and he, too, left the small room.

"Come on." Sara Beth pulled a clean gown out of a cabinet and set it on the examining table next to Lisa's legs. She held the ice pack against the back of Lisa's head as she sat up and began undoing the buttons on her blouse.

"How long was I out?"

"Long enough to have everyone worried." Sara Beth took Lisa's blouse and bra when she slid them off and handed her the cotton gown. "You didn't even come to when I did a blood draw."

Lisa stared at her arm, noticing for the first time the little adhesive bandage holding a wad of cotton in the fold of her elbow. An exam maybe wasn't such a bad idea.

She slid gingerly off the table and toed off her pumps, then slid off her wide-legged pants. She realized that they were the pants she'd worn the day she'd met Rourke at Fare.

Her chest squeezed. She finished undressing and yanked the thin gown together, trying not to shiver in the room that, until that moment, had seemed overly warm.

"I need to get a chart started for you. I'll be right back." Sara Beth handed her the ice pack and let herself out of the examining room.

Lisa sat on the table, holding the pack against the back of her head, and looked down at the cotton crumpled across her belly. "Don't be scaring us like this," she whispered.

Then Sara Beth came back, asking about a hundred questions as she began filling out the medical chart. She took Lisa's blood pressure. Waved her out into the empty hall between examining rooms and made her stand on the scale. Then back into the room again. "I'll get Chance."

Sara Beth returned with the doctor within minutes and Lisa found herself answering a good portion of the questions that Sara Beth had already asked. By the time Chance finished examining her, she knew firsthand just how thorough the man was.

"Everything looks good," he said, when he took the chart from Sara Beth and began scribbling on it. "We'll schedule you for an ultrasound week after next. I think you're too early yet to have a good result. You'll start on prenatal vitamins immediately." He slanted a stern look at her. "And you'll beef up your diet. You're too thin." He tore off a page from his prescription pad and handed it to her. "I think our biggest concern is the conk on your head. So don't be alone for the next twenty-four hours. Dizziness. Vision problems. Nausea. Watch for them. And obviously call me immediately if you start spotting or cramping."

"I'll stay with you," Sara Beth offered even before Lisa could form a protest about the twenty-four-hour bit.

"Otherwise—" he grinned at her "—congratulations, Mom."

Lisa smile weakly. He was clearly aware that his and Ted's treatment of Rourke had led to her pregnancy. "Thanks." She folded the prescription into neat halves after he left. "I don't need help getting dressed, Sara Beth. This place is busting at the seams with patients. Paying ones."

"True enough. I'll just nip next door for a sec. If you get dizzy again, lie down." Sara Beth closed the file folder and took it with her.

Lisa slid off the table. The only thing plaguing her was the dull throb in her head but even that had begun to ease. She pushed the gown into the basket in the corner for just that purpose, and began dressing again. She was just buttoning up her blouse when she heard the door crack open. "I'm fine, Sara Beth," she said, without looking. "Go see your next patient."

"It's not Sara Beth."

She started so violently, the tiny pearl button she was trying to slip through the hole pulled off right in her hand. She rounded on her heel to face Rourke.

He looked dreadful. As if he hadn't slept in days. His face was lined. His charcoal suit was wrinkled and his tie was hanging askew.

"What are you doing here?"

"Ted called me. Said you'd fainted."

She steeled herself against feeling anything. "Convenient that you were in town, then." Her voice was cool.

"I wasn't." His gaze was roving over her. "I was at my office." His lips twisted. "Not that I was doing anything productive there. What happened?"

She looked at the clock on the wall. If he'd only left since Ted had called him, he'd made the fastest commute from New York to Boston known to man. "I got dizzy." She turned her back on him to finish buttoning her blouse. It was probably ludicrous, considering the man knew her body even better than she did, but it still made her feel better. "Don't worry. Your investment is still secure."

"Don't." His voice was low. Rough. "Don't act like that's all this is to me. You know better."

The throbbing in her chest outdid the throbbing in her head by a mile. She couldn't do anything about the missing button just above the low band at the center of her bra, so she left the two above it open, as well. She shoved the silk shirttails into her pants and began fastening the wide belt. "I certainly know enough." She pushed her feet into her pumps and turned to face him, feeling more armored with her clothing intact. "Now, that is."

"You don't know that I fell in love with you."

She'd underestimated his ability to hurt her any more than she was already hurting. And the blow of that shook her through to her soul.

She couldn't move forward to the door to escape the small room without brushing against him. So she did the only thing she could do. "You don't have to lie to me now, Rourke. You've got what you wanted. You've pulverized an Armstrong like you were pulverized and in less than eight months, you'll have the heir you'd feared you'd never have. All in a day's work for you. Well. I guess a few weeks more than a day. But still—" her lips twisted "—well done."

"I haven't got what I want. I haven't got you."

Her heart felt as if it was splintering. "What more do you want from us?" The ice in her voice was breaking into chunks. "Derek was right. You own more of the Armstrong Fertility Institute now than any of the Armstrongs do. What else is left for you to take?"

"I'm not trying to take anything. For the first time in a long time, I'm trying to give something!" His voice rose and he exhaled through his clenched teeth. He yanked an envelope out of his lapel pocket and tossed it on the end of the leather-covered examining table. "There. Take it. Do whatever the hell you want with it."

She stared at the envelope as if it was a snake. "What is it?"

"The prenup."

A snake, indeed. But she snatched up the envelope anyway. Pulled out the lengthy document that had outlined the terms of their agreement. She tossed it back on the table. "I'm sure you have copies."

"Is there nothing that you can let yourself trust me about?" His voice was tight. "That's the original. The only copy. You can tear it up. Walk away from me. Take half of everything I've ever worked for, but you're not going to do it without knowing the truth."

"Truth!" Her arms lifted. "I learned the truth on the sidewalk outside your building last night! I was the perfect tool for you, wasn't I? Dedicated-to-the-institute Lisa. Who'd do anything to keep her father's legacy alive, even though her father turns out to be as fallible as the rest of us. Who was too backward when it came to men to realize just how well she was being played. What an ideal setup it was for you, and you didn't even have to chase it down. *I* came to *you!*"

"I should have told you about Taylor and your brother. About everything. Including the treatment." His voice sounded like gravel. "But in the beginning, it didn't matter. And in the end, it mattered too much."

"Stop." She lifted her hand. "The day we got married, you said I'd at least have respect. So allow me that and stop…pretending…that you feel anything other than accomplishment." Her vision was wavering again, only this time it was due to tears. She flicked her finger against the wrinkled folds of the prenup. "As far as I'm concerned, everything in there still stands. You fund the institute in exchange for the child we'll share custody of." Blocking the door or not, she had to get out of there. She headed past him. "There's nothing else I want from you.

He shot out an arm, blocking her. "Too bad," he said unevenly. "Because you've got my heart. And believe me, princess, until you came along, I didn't know there was one left to give. Maybe we didn't start out the way we should have. But that doesn't lessen the way I feel now. I never meant to hurt you. Throw it back in my face if you have to, but I'm not letting you go until you at least believe in that."

He was hurting her now, by preventing her escape. And she couldn't even maintain the pretense that she wasn't utterly destroyed. "Please," she whispered. "Don't do this to me. I...can't bear any more."

"And I can't bear to let you walk away from me." His hands closed tightly around her shoulders. "Not again. And that has *nothing* to do with the baby we've made."

She closed her eyes. Looked away from him. "If I didn't look like her would you have ever even agreed to meet with me when Ted asked you to?"

"I've never mistaken you for Taylor." His voice dropped. "You weren't a substitute. You could never be a substitute for anyone. I wouldn't want you to be. You're entirely unique and the way I feel about you isn't in the same universe as what I felt for her. The only thing she took with her when I told her we were through was some of my pride. And I may have let that rule me for too long afterward, but I don't give a damn about my pride now."

She could feel his hands shaking as they moved from her shoulders to her face as he lifted it until she had to look at him.

His eyes were bloodshot. And they were wet.

"I don't have any pride that matters when it comes to you." His voice was as raw as his expression. "What I feel for you isn't about the baby. Or proving that I'm man enough to give you one. And it isn't about extracting some revenge that I don't even care about anymore. It's about you. And me. And the fact that when I'm with you, the only thing I care about is *staying* with you. Going to bed at night, knowing you'll still be mine when I wake up the next morning. Even when we're in different freaking cities. It's about sharing what's in your head and in your heart. It's about the fact that you've crawled inside here." He slapped his hand against his chest. "And I can't get you out." He exhaled roughly. "And I don't want to."

She stared at him, tears sliding silently down her face.

"Everything my mother raised me to believe that matters—children, family—is what brought us here. Whether I was right or wrong in the process. But right now, if I could take away the baby inside you just to prove that it is you that matters most of all, I would. But I can't. And I can't pretend I don't want our child more than I want my next breath. But it's because he or she is *ours.*"

She sucked in a sob. "Rourke."

"All I can do is ask you to believe me. Believe *in* me. I love you. But if you can tell me right now that you don't love me, I'll let you go. Just as I promised the day we got married. But I won't be able to take back my heart." His jaw twisted to one side. "Because that is always going to be yours."

She stepped back from him. Saw the way the blood blanched from his haggard face.

Then she deliberately picked up the prenup and tore it in half. Then half again before she let the ruined squares flutter to the floor. "I love you, too." Her voice was raw. "And I don't want to go anywhere that would take me away from you."

He closed his eyes for a long moment.

Then he looked at her. Caught her left hand in his and slowly lifted it. He kissed the wedding rings she hadn't been able to make herself take off.

She bit her lip, her heart as open to him as the palm of her hand when he slowly turned it over to press his lips there.

Then he was pulling her to him, lifting her off her feet, his arms nearly crushing her ribs as his mouth found hers.

And there, in her husband's arms with his heart thundering against hers, she realized she'd been wrong.

Fairy tales *could* come true.

Sara Beth opened the door behind them, and smiled tremulously at the sight. Just as quietly, she closed the door once again. There was no need for her to worry about Lisa's next twenty-four hours after all.

Epilogue

"Happy birthday, Daddy." Ignoring the decidedly pinched look on her mother's face where she stood beside Gerald, Lisa leaned over her father's wheelchair and pressed a kiss to his lined cheek, very aware of the attention on them from the family members gathered in the drawing room behind her.

Among them were not only her original siblings, but her newfound one, as well. Lisa had insisted that Sara Beth and Ted join the family for the private dinner they were having before the rest of the guests arrived later that evening.

Sara Beth had reluctantly agreed, but only after insisting that Lisa confirm with both Paul and Olivia that they had no objection. Fortunately, her brother and sister had treated the news that Sara Beth was their sibling with more equanimity than Lisa had.

They'd immediately agreed that she and Ted should be there. And that evening, when he and Sara Beth had arrived at the Armstrong house, it was Olivia who'd beaten Lisa to the punch, giving Sara Beth a hug and pulling her into the study where Emily and Gerald had yet to join them. "Come and say hello to my sons. Your nephews."

Lisa smiled and leaned back against Rourke's shoulder, watching them. She felt the kiss he brushed across her temple, though his present debate with Jamison on some political point didn't hesitate for a moment. Then Paul and Ramona arrived. And he, too, headed immediately for Sara Beth. "I always did say you looked like that portrait of our grandmother," he greeted her and tugged her into his arms for a kiss. "Welcome to the family." He grinned a little crookedly. "For what it's worth."

"Thank you." Sara Beth's gaze found Lisa's. "It's worth quite a lot, actually."

"Drinks, anyone?" Jamison ambled to the bar.

"Fruit juice for Sara Beth and Lisa," Olivia inserted, her gaze twinkling. She joined her tall husband, looking up at him with nothing but delight in her expression. "No wine for the pregnant duo."

"Ramona? What about you?"

"Fruit juice will do for me, too."

Everyone stopped dead still, looking across at her. She laughed outright, particularly at Paul's stunned expression. "Don't worry," she assured them. "I'm just getting in practice. For *after* the wedding."

Paul let out an audible breath and everyone laughed.

Until they'd noticed Emily pushing Gerald's chair through the doorway.

And the fact that Derek was walking behind them.

Rourke had stiffened behind her, but he'd said nothing. Nor had Paul or Olivia.

And Lisa had finally taken the bull by the horns and walked

over to her father. "Happy birthday, Daddy." She straightened and pressed a second kiss to her mother's cheek. "Mother. You look lovely tonight."

Emily couldn't hide the surprise that flitted across her face. "Thank you, dear. So do you. I hear from Paul that congratulations are in order." If she was hurt that Lisa hadn't told her about her pregnancy herself, she hid it well. "Are you feeling all right?"

"Never better," she assured her truthfully. Even with the nausea that had started plaguing her in the mornings, she had never felt better in her life. How could she not?

Rourke loved her. And she loved him.

"You can see that I've asked Sara Beth to join us."

Emily's lips pinched together again. "Clearly." Her chin lifted a little. "And you all can see that your father and I have asked Derek to be here." She drew him forward.

He looked only marginally better than he had when he'd shown up outside Rourke's apartment. Still too pale and much too thin. But his eyes were clear and steady and they met Lisa's head on. "Lisa."

Lisa felt Rourke come up beside her. His hand slipped protectively around her shoulder.

For a moment, Derek looked as if he wanted to turn around and leave. But he stood his ground. "Devlin."

"Derek."

Gerald cleared his throat, breaking the barely civil tension. "Before anyone says anything else, I have something to say." Waving off Emily's aid, he wheeled his chair into the center of the room. "Derek's told your mother and me everything." He closed his unsteady hands together. "About the embezzlement." He looked at Paul. "The real reason you told him to leave the institute." He looked at Lisa. "Which finally explains why your husband's money was suddenly fueling our coffers.

And while that grieves me—us—deeply, what grieves me more is that none of you thought fit to come and tell me what was going on when it was going on. I had to find out about it when Derek's counselor at the rehab clinic he checked himself into called me."

"Daddy," Lisa said, "your health has been—"

"Bad." Gerald nodded. "Nobody knows that better than me. So you were trying to protect me." His gaze drifted to Sara Beth. "And Emily's tried to protect me. Protect her family."

"Gerald—"

"Enough, Emily. I've had enough. I'm not dead and in the grave yet and I'm going to have my say and then that'll be the end of it."

Emily blinked. Closed her delicately gaping mouth.

"The institute has weathered a lot this past year," Gerald said. "This *family* has weathered a lot. For a lot longer than just a year or two and Lord knows that I bear the responsibility for most of that." His gaze touched on Olivia and Jamison and their two new sons. Moved on to Sara Beth and Ted, whose arms were looped protectively around her. Then Paul and Ramona, and Lisa and Rourke, before settling on his wife again. "Nobody's perfect."

Derek's face flushed a little, but he didn't look down, or away.

"Least of all me," Gerald added. "But it's time to stop moaning over the past and *do better* for the future." He held out his hand toward Emily and she looked thoroughly unsettled as she moved forward to take it. "The fact of the matter is, both the institute and this family are still going on. The institute will be better than ever. And this family is going to *be* a family. All of us." There was steel in his voice. The kind of steel that Lisa hadn't heard in a very long time. "Are we agreed?" He looked at his wife. "Emily?"

She looked almost teary. "Yes, dear. Agreed."

He nodded. "All right, then." His voice went a little gruff and he cleared his throat. "Happy birthday to me. So let's eat before the staff and the rest of the city descends on us since I figure that's about how many people my wife has invited to celebrate the fact that I'm getting to be as old as Methuselah."

"Oh, Gerald." Cleary flustered, Emily took his chair and began wheeling him out of the room.

Derek's gaze ran over the rest of them. "For what it's worth, I am sorry." His voice was low.

Even across the room, Lisa could hear Paul exhale. Then he was drawing Ramona forward and he closed his hand over his twin's shoulder. "You heard Dad," he said gruffly. "Let's go eat."

Lisa watched them follow her parents. Olivia and her crew went behind and she was drawing Sara Beth along with her, wanting to know when the baby was due.

The last ones left in the drawing room, Lisa looked up at Rourke. "Can you stand to sit at the same table as Derek?"

"The only thing I care about is whether you can sit at the same table as your brother."

Just when she thought her heart couldn't pump out any more love for him than it already did, it leaked some more. "I can." She started to follow after the others, but Rourke reeled her back to him before she got more than an arm's distance.

"Your father *is* impressive," he murmured.

"He is." She smiled faintly. "Thank you."

A faint smile played around his lips. His gaze was as warm on her face as the hands linked behind her back that held her against his broad chest. "For what?"

"Loving me."

His lips grazed over hers. "I could no more stop that, than I could stop breathing."

"Good." She kissed him back. "But if you do…" She leaned up until her lips were inches from his ear. "Just remember, there's always a doctor around in this family who knows CPR. They'll keep you breathing one way or another."

He threw his head back and laughed. He pressed a hard, thorough kiss on her lips. "That's my girl."

She smiled at him, so deeply happy that it invaded her every cell.

Yes. She was his girl. And even when they were old and gray and their children had children of their own, she knew in her bones that was what she would always be.

And still smiling, fingers twining together, they went out and joined the rest of the family.

* * * * *

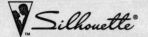

COMING NEXT MONTH

Available June 29, 2010

#2053 McFARLANE'S PERFECT BRIDE
Christine Rimmer
Montana Mavericks: Thunder Canyon Cowboys

#2054 WELCOME HOME, COWBOY
Karen Templeton
Wed in the West

#2055 ACCIDENTAL FATHER
Nancy Robards Thompson

#2056 THE BABY SURPRISE
Brenda Harlen
Brides & Babies

#2057 THE DOCTOR'S UNDOING
Gina Wilkins
Doctors in Training

#2058 THE BOSS'S PROPOSAL
Kristin Hardy
The McBains of Grace Harbor

SPECIAL EDITION

SSECNM0610

HARLEQUIN®

A Romance

FOR EVERY MOOD™

Spotlight on
Heart & Home

Heartwarming romances
where love can happen
right when you least expect it.

See the next page to enjoy a sneak peek
from Silhouette Special Edition®,
a Heart and Home series.

Introducing McFARLANE'S PERFECT BRIDE
by USA TODAY *bestselling author Christine Rimmer,*
from Silhouette Special Edition®.

Entranced. Captivated. Enchanted.

Connor sat across the table from Tori Jones and couldn't help thinking that those words exactly described what effect the small-town schoolteacher had on him. He might as well stop trying to tell himself he wasn't interested. He was powerfully drawn to her.

Clearly, he should have dated more when he was younger.

There had been a couple of other women since Jennifer had walked out on him. But he had never been entranced. Or captivated. Or enchanted.

Until now.

He wanted her—*her,* Tori Jones, in particular. Not just someone suitably attractive and well-bred, as Jennifer had been. Not just someone sophisticated, sexually exciting and discreet, which pretty much described the two women he'd dated after his marriage crashed and burned.

It came to him that he…he *liked* this woman. And that was new to him. He liked her quick wit, her wisdom and her big heart. He liked the passion in her voice when she talked about things she believed in.

He liked *her.* And suddenly it mattered all out of proportion that she might like him, too.

Was he losing it? He couldn't help but wonder. Was he cracking under the strain—of the soured economy, the McFarlane House setbacks, his divorce, the scary changes in his son? Of the changes he'd decided he needed to make in his life and himself?

Strangely, right then, on his first date with Tori Jones, he didn't care if he just might be going over the edge. He was having a great time—having *fun*, of all things—and he didn't want it to end.

Is Connor finally able to admit his feelings to Tori,
and are they reciprocated?
Find out in McFARLANE'S PERFECT BRIDE
by USA TODAY *bestselling author Christine Rimmer.*
Available July 2010,
only from Silhouette Special Edition®.

SSEEXP0710

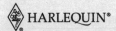

HARLEQUIN®

Showcase

LESLIE KELLY
Naturally Naughty

Wicked & Willing

On sale June 8

Reader favorites from the most talented voices in romance

Save $1.00 on the purchase of 1 or more Harlequin® Showcase books.

SAVE $1.00

on the purchase of 1 or more Harlequin® Showcase books.

Coupon expires November 30, 2010. Redeemable at participating retail outlets.
Limit one coupon per customer. Valid in the U.S.A. and Canada only.

Canadian Retailers: Harlequin Enterprises Limited will pay the face value of this coupon plus 10.25¢ if submitted by customer for this product only. Any other use constitutes fraud. Coupon is nonassignable. Void if taxed, prohibited or restricted by law. Consumer must pay any government taxes. Void if copied. Nielsen Clearing House ("NCH") customers submit coupons and proof of sales to Harlequin Enterprises Limited, P.O. Box 3000, Saint John, NB E2L 4L3, Canada. Non-NCH retailer—for reimbursement submit coupons and proof of sales directly to Harlequin Enterprises Limited, Retail Marketing Department, 225 Duncan Mill Rd., Don Mills, ON M3B 3K9, Canada.

U.S. Retailers: Harlequin Enterprises Limited will pay the face value of this coupon plus 8¢ if submitted by customer for this product only. Any other use constitutes fraud. Coupon is nonassignable. Void if taxed, prohibited or restricted by law. Consumer must pay any government taxes. Void if copied. For reimbursement submit coupons and proof of sales directly to Harlequin Enterprises Limited, P.O. Box 880478, El Paso, TX 88588-0478, U.S.A. Cash value 1/100 cents.

52609057

5 65373 00076 2   (8100)0 11654

® and TM are trademarks owned and used by the trademark owner and/or its licensee.
© 2010 Harlequin Enterprises Limited

HSCCOUP0610